Abby and the Mystery Baby

**Other books by
Ann M. Martin**

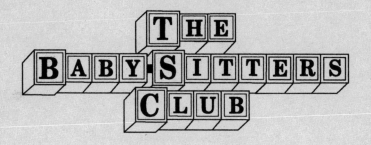

Abby and the Mystery Baby
Ann M. Martin

AN
APPLE
PAPERBACK

SCHOLASTIC INC.
New York Toronto London Auckland Sydney

Cover art by Hodges Soileau

ISBN 0-590-69176-7

12 11 10 9 8 7 6 5 4 3 2 1   7 8 9/9 0 1 2/0

Printed in the U.S.A.   40

First Scholastic printing, February 1997

*The author gratefully acknowledges
Ellen Miles
for her help in
preparing this manuscript.*

Abby and the Mystery Baby

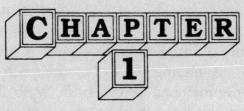

CHAPTER 1

"Go, Abby!"

"Move it, Stevenson!"

"Looking good!"

I didn't even break my stride when I heard the yelling. I just grinned and stuck both thumbs up in the air. Then, out of the corner of my eye, I saw the big yellow blur of a school bus trundling by me. The bus was full of kids, and some of them (the ones who'd pulled down their windows to shout at me) were friends. They were on their way home from school, and so was I. The difference was that I had chosen to run rather than ride.

I knew my friends thought I was nuts. After all, it was wintertime and not exactly warm out. Why would anyone choose a sweaty, gasping run over a comfy ride on the bus?

The thing is, even though they are my friends, none of those kids knows me very well. That's because I moved here ("here" is

1

Stoneybrook, Connecticut) only recently. Back at my old school, on Long Island, nobody would have been surprised to see me running at this time of year.

"There goes Abby," they'd say. "Training, as usual."

As my old friends know — and as my new friends are finding out — I'm always in training for something. Soccer, track, softball, you name it. Not that I think sports are everything. I have plenty of other interests. But being in good shape physically is important to me.

Hold on. Here I am, babbling on, and we haven't even been formally introduced. Well, let's back up, then. My name's Abby Stevenson. I'm thirteen years old and I'm in eighth grade at Stoneybrook Middle School. I have a twin sister named Anna, and we live with our mom in a house that's really a bit too big for the three of us.

There used to be four of us, but that was before we moved to Stoneybrook, back when Anna and I were kids, when my mom was a happy, relaxed kind of person who laughed a lot and cooked the most incredible food. (She was going to cooking school at the time, to learn how to be a chef.)

That was before my dad died.

I don't talk about him much, so I'm only going to say this once: My dad was the best. He was the one who made my mom laugh. He was an environmental engineer with the heart of a hippie (he went to the original Woodstock!). He cared about the world and about making it a better place. He gave the best hugs. He played the harmonica — not well, but I'd give him an E for effort. He wore steel-rimmed glasses and plaid flannel shirts, and he always smelled good.

And then one day he was gone. He died in a car accident when Anna and I were nine, and nothing has ever been the same.

My mom changed her job and became a high-powered editor at a publishing house in New York City. Recently, she was promoted, and since we could afford it, we moved to a nicer, bigger house here in Connecticut. I like Stoneybrook just fine, and I've made some good friends here. I've even become a member of this terrific club called the BSC, or Baby-sitters Club (more about that later).

But I'll never stop missing my dad.

Neither will Anna. She's made friends here too. They're mostly music friends. Anna is an incredibly talented musician who spends nearly all of her free time practicing the violin. She's in the orchestra at school, and she also takes private lessons and plays chamber music with other musicians.

As you've probably guessed, Anna and I are

pretty different as far as personality goes. We do look alike, though. We both have dark, dark brown eyes — they're almost black, really — and terrible eyesight, which we correct with contacts and glasses (not at the same time, naturally). And we have the same thick, curly, dark hair.

We recently discovered one other physical difference between us: Anna has scoliosis, which is curvature of the spine. Her curve is pretty minor, and she won't need surgery. But she does have to wear a brace for awhile.

At first I was worried about Anna. I hovered around trying to take care of her and cheer her up, instead of letting her work through things on her own. I nearly drove her crazy. We even had a big fight about it. But once we sorted it all out, we ended up closer than ever.

I love being a twin. Anna and I are connected forever in some very deep and mysterious ways. At times, when we're separated, we'll have these *feelings* about each other. And they'll turn out to be true. For instance, one time, I was having this monster asthma attack and Anna knew it, even though she was miles away at an all-state orchestra competition.

Asthma. The bane of my existence. Did you ever have the feeling that you needed air desperately, but no matter what you did you couldn't seem to pull enough of it into your lungs? Probably not, unless you are a fellow asthmatic. All I can tell you is that it's the pits. I don't let it keep me from doing things, though. I carry inhalers with me at all times, and if I feel a little short of breath or a bit wheezy, they usually fix me right up. Usually. Not always. There have been a couple of trips to the emergency room, but I prefer not to think about those.

I also have mondo allergies to dogs, kitty litter (but not cats, oddly enough), any kind of dust, pillows with feathers in them (ooh, just thinking about that can make me sneeze!), and a bunch of different foods, including shellfish and cheese. It's a drag, but what can you do? I've learned to live with my allergies and asthma, though I keep hoping I'll grow out of them sometime.

Thump, thump, thump. My running shoes made a satisfying rhythm as they hit the sidewalk. My arms pumped easily, my breathing was deep and regular, and I felt relaxed and happy. Running always makes me feel good. I was glad I'd decided it was time to quit riding and start striding.

I smiled as I ran, thinking about how I'd cracked up my table in the cafeteria during lunch hour. I'd been doing impressions of our teachers, and of Mr. Kingbridge, the assistant principal. I'm a pretty good mimic, if I do say so myself. I'm never mean about it; I don't pick on people's speech impediments or anything. I just try to copy their walks, their ways of gesturing, their particular speech patterns, and soon my audience is practically rolling on the floor.

Back in my old school, I had a name as a class clown. It hasn't taken long to build the same reputation here in Stoneybrook. I'm always the first to fire off a one-liner or perform a little bit of slapstick. And truthfully? I don't think the teachers mind it. I notice they're usually smiling, too. After all, who couldn't use a little humor in the day?

Anyway, it's not as if I use comedy to avoid my schoolwork. I'm a decent student, and I usually make better-than-average grades, as long as I'm not stressed out. For instance, the way I was not long ago when Anna and I were studying for our Bat Mitzvah.

"Bat what?" you might be asking. Don't worry, I'll explain. See, my family is Jewish, and when Jewish girls turn thirteen they take part in a special celebration called a Bat Mitzvah. (Boys have a celebration, too, called a Bar Mitzvah.) It's a big deal, because it represents a person's entry into adulthood.

The thing is, it's not just a party. It's much more than that. When you become a Bat Mitzvah, you have to read (in public) from a scroll called the Torah. Which is written in Hebrew. Yikes. So, for about a year before the big day, Anna and I had to study Hebrew. Plus, we each had to write a speech, which we would give after our Torah readings. The speech was the part that pushed me over the edge in the days leading up to our Bat Mitzvah. It was a nightmare, but somehow it all worked out and I made it through the day with flying colors.

Just thinking about our Bat Mitzvah made me grateful for having nothing bigger to worry about than what to eat for a snack when I arrived at home.

Thump, thump, thump. I really had a great rhythm going now. I looked around at the patches of snow and the bare brown branches of the trees (soon to be covered with green) and thought about how nice it used to be back when Mom was going to cooking school. I'd arrive home after school to find her in the kitchen, doing "homework."

"What do you think of this puff pastry?" she'd ask, shoving a tray of gorgeous, chocolate-drizzled treats at me. "Try the one on the left and tell me if you think it's flakier than the one on the right."

"Mmmpph," I'd say, after I'd taken a few bites (just to be polite, of course). "They're both awesome."

Those were the days. Now when I walk into

the house, I'm more than likely to find a chilly, empty kitchen. I'm always the first one home, since Anna is either at orchestra or lessons or some other music-related activity. And Mom? Mom commutes by train to her job in New York City, where she almost always works late. If she makes it home before seven it's an event. We rarely eat a home-cooked meal together on weekdays. The three of us subsist on frozen dinners, pizza, and take-out Chinese.

So, as far as afternoon snacks go, let's just say that the microwave and I have become very, very close pals. And I don't even mind the empty house so much anymore. I'm used to it, I guess.

I was feeling great as I turned into our U-shaped driveway. There's nothing like a good, brisk run to make you feel pumped up and happy. I'd decided I was going to nuke a bean burrito for my snack, and I was looking forward to the quiet couple of hours I'd have before my BSC meeting later that afternoon.

I trotted up the driveway, slowing my pace in order to cool down a little before my postrun stretching routine. I usually stretch on our front porch, which is humongous. As I approached, I saw a bulky, light-colored object near the front door. (It stood out because the door, which is beautifully carved, is made out of dark wood.) Was it a package? Maybe it was

8

the bike helmet I'd ordered. That would be excellent. But as I drew closer, I saw that it wasn't a package at all.

It was a car seat. A small, gray one. The kind people use for babies. It was just sitting there on the porch, which I thought was weird. Why would someone leave a car seat on our front porch? Forgetting about my stretching routine, I stepped up onto the porch to take a look.

The car seat wasn't empty.

There was a baby in it. A living, breathing, squirming baby — about four months old, to my expert baby-sitter's eye.

Someone had left a baby on our doorstep.

CHAPTER 2

Panic city.

I took a deep breath. Then I took a couple more. I stared at the baby, and it stared calmly back at me with huge, slate-blue eyes that matched its little blue hat and also the blue cowboys and horses on the threadbare — but clean — red blanket that it was wrapped in.

"Who *are* you?" I said out loud. "And why on earth would anyone leave you here?" The baby blinked, but other than that its serene expression didn't change. And it certainly didn't speak up with an answer to my questions.

I shivered a little. I'd been plenty warm during my run, but now I realized that it wasn't exactly balmy out. "Well, whoever you are, I think you'd better come inside with me," I said. I opened the front door, gathered up the car seat, went inside, and kicked the door shut behind me.

The house was empty. Big surprise, right? As I said, I've grown used to being the first one home. But that day, I felt more alone than ever. It was just me and the baby, and, more than anything, I wished someone else were there to help me figure out what to do.

"Anna?" I called tentatively. Maybe, just maybe, she'd decided to skip orchestra for once.

No such luck.

"Mom?" I tried. My voice sounded a little shaky.

The silence was broken only by a little sniff. I looked down and saw that the baby looked as if it were about to sneeze.

"Okay, baby," I said, heading toward the living room. My arms were tired from holding the car seat, and I needed to put it down. "It's just you and me. Let's make ourselves comfortable." I settled the car seat onto the couch. The baby, still calm, gazed at me as I stripped off my warm-up jacket and kicked off my running shoes.

I sat down on the couch to take a closer look at this tiny person who had appeared on my doorstep. One little arm had wiggled free of the blanket and was waving around. "You are *adorable*," I said, picking up the tiny hand and looking at the even tinier, perfect fingernails that adorned it. The hand was warm. The baby couldn't have been out on that porch for very long.

The baby frowned.

"And I bet you'd like to get out of that car seat, wouldn't you?" I asked. Carefully, moving slowly so as not to startle the baby, I unfastened the strap that held it securely into the seat. Then I picked up the baby, blanket and all. "Ohhh." I sighed as I pulled the baby close for a hug. Its warm weight filled my arms, and I could smell that delicious baby smell coming from the top of its head.

There was another smell, too. It was faint but unmistakable. The baby needed its diaper changed. How was I supposed to deal with *that*? I felt the panic rise again. Then I took a deep breath and tried to calm down.

I glanced back at the car seat and noticed a navy blue bag that must have been wedged in next to the baby. With any luck, it would hold clean diapers. I shifted the baby's weight to one arm, reached over, and retrieved the bag. Sure enough, it was packed full of diapers, wipes, formula, bottles, and even a couple of clean sleepers. This baby came fully equipped. Obviously, someone cared about this child. But why had he (or she) abandoned the baby, and why on *my* porch?

I went to work right there on the couch. I unwrapped the blanket to find that the baby was dressed in a yellow sleeper with ducklings embroidered on it. "Oh, how cute!" I said. Laying the baby down on the blanket, I unsnapped the legs of its sleeper and saw a pretty soggy disposable diaper. I pulled it off.

Suddenly, I had an answer to something I'd been wondering about.

"A boy!" I said. "He's a liddle, iddle boy." I knew I sounded ridiculous, but nobody was there to hear me. Except the baby. Who was now smiling up at me.

He was too cute for words.

I wiped him down, fastened on a clean, dry diaper, and snapped the legs of his suit up again. "There you go, sir!" I said. "All set."

He smiled again, and my heart melted. I bent down and rubbed noses with him. "You are the bestest, sweetest, oogiest little booger I ever saw," I murmured to him. Something about babies just brings out those nonsense words, doesn't it?

The baby squirmed and gave a tiny hiccup. Then he smiled again.

I was in love.

I was also awfully curious. Who was this gorgeous little guy? Who had put him on my porch, and why? And why *my* porch? For one crazy second, I had this image of the stork getting lost and leaving this baby with us by mistake. Like in *Dumbo*.

That was a nutty idea, but it was nicer than some of the other ideas that were popping into my head. Like, had the baby been kidnapped? Was his mom crying her eyes out, wondering where he was? Who *was* his mom, and how would I ever find her?

Just then the phone rang and I crash-landed back into reality.

I picked up the baby and ran for the phone. "Hello?" I said, hoping against hope that it would be my mother or some other responsible adult. I suddenly realized that I had no idea what to do next. I mean, a baby had landed on my doorstep, a baby I knew nothing about. What was I supposed to *do?*

"Mrs. Stevenson?" asked a voice on the other end. A calm, female voice.

"No, this is *Ms.* Stevenson," I said. "Who is this?"

"I'm calling from Benco Industries," the woman said. "With a very special offer just for the Stevenson family."

Oh, brother. A sales call. My heart sank. But the woman sounded so nice and so capable. For a second, I had the urge to blurt out my problem. ("See, this baby just arrived on my doorstep and . . .") but I realized how ridicu-

14

lous that would be. This lady on the other end of the phone couldn't help me, even if she did sound wise and comforting.

"Thank you, but I'm really not interested," I said. "Good-bye." As I hung up the phone, something caught my eye. A piece of paper lay near the sugar bowl on the kitchen table. I picked it up. It was a note from my mom.

"Came home from work early," it said. "Heating system broke and it was freezing there. Out doing errands."

That meant Mom would be home soon. Yes! But there was no knowing exactly when. Boo!

And I needed help *now*. Help figuring out what to do. I was so panicked I just couldn't think straight. I shifted the baby from one arm to the other as I gazed at the phone. Who could I call?

Kristy. That was it. Kristy Thomas knows what to do in any situation. Kristy's a friend, a neighbor, and the president of the BSC. I knew she could help. I dialed her number.

Kristy appeared at my front door approximately six seconds after we'd hung up. Behind her was her grandmother, Nannie.

"Oh, look at the poor little guy," cooed Nannie, holding out her arms for the baby. "What a tiny thing, to be away from his parents." I handed him over, and she immediately started making those "oogie, boogie" noises to him. I guess it's universal.

Kristy, meanwhile, swung into action. "What time did you come home?" she asked. "And where was he, exactly? And was there any kind of note or I.D.?" The questions tumbled out of her so quickly I could barely keep up.

"Um, I guess about half an hour ago. On the porch. No. Not that I saw." I was a little dazed.

"Okay, let's make the call," said Kristy, marching into the kitchen.

"The call?" I asked, following her and feeling stupid.

But Kristy wasn't waiting for me to figure it out. She'd already dialed. "Sergeant Johnson, please," she said crisply into the phone. Then she said a bunch of other stuff, but I missed most of it, because just then my mom came home.

"Hi, sweetie," she called, hurrying into the kitchen and stripping off her gloves. The baby chose that moment to begin shrieking at the top of his liddle, iddle lungs.

"What — ?" asked my mother, her mouth open wide and her eyebrows raised high.

The baby screamed even more loudly, and Nannie appeared in the kitchen doorway, holding him. "I think he's hungry," she said apologetically.

16

"There's formula in the blue bag," I said, trying to be heard over his cries.

"Blue bag? Formula?" asked my mother. "What's going *on?*"

For a few minutes everything was chaos as Kristy, Nannie, and I tried to explain things to my mom, find the formula, heat it, make up a bottle, and settle the baby down to drink it.

"Is this the blanket the baby came wrapped in?" asked my mother, when we'd all trooped back into the living room. Her voice sounded a little strange.

"Yes, and I know it's kind of thin," I said, "but he really wasn't cold. Whoever left him made sure he'd be all right."

My mother muttered something, but I didn't quite catch it. She folded the blanket carefully and spent some time tucking it back into the car seat. Then she leaned over to take another, closer look at the baby, who was lying peacefully in Nannie's arms, content now that he had a bottle to suck on. I saw my mother's face soften as she gazed at the baby, but she looked worried, too.

There was a knock at the door. "That must be Sergeant Johnson," said Kristy, jumping up to answer it. Sure enough, when she returned she was accompanied by a tall policeman with black hair and clear blue eyes.

Sergeant Johnson is a great guy. The BSC has

helped to solve more than one mystery in Stoneybrook, and Sergeant Johnson has become our friend.

"Well, well, would you look at him," said Sergeant Johnson, after all the introductions had been made. He gave the baby a little chuck under the chin and made some "oogie, boogie" noises. (Why wasn't I surprised?)

Then Anna came home, and we had to explain everything all over again and listen to more "oogie, boogies." By that time the living room was full of people.

"I'd like to talk to each of you in turn," said Sergeant Johnson, pulling a small notebook out of his shirt pocket. "Okay if we use the kitchen?" he asked my mom. She nodded, and Sergeant Johnson turned to me. "You were the first one to find him, right? Let's go."

He led me into the kitchen, asked me to sit, and listened as I told him every detail I could remember. He wrote it all down and sent me back to the living room for Kristy. I was still a little dazed, but it sure felt good to have someone else take charge.

We all sat in the living room, looking at the baby and handing him around, as each person was called into the kitchen to talk to Sergeant Johnson. My mom was last. I went into the kitchen to heat up more formula, just as she was finishing up, and heard Sergeant Johnson saying, "I see. Well, that *could* be possible. Of course we'll follow every lead." My ears pricked up, but before I could ask what lead my mother had suggested, Kristy poked her head into the room.

"It's time for the BSC meeting," she said. "I'll call Charlie and ask him to swing by." (Charlie, one of Kristy's older brothers, drives us to BSC meetings.) She headed for the phone. "You don't have to come if you don't want to. I'd understand."

"Actually, I'd like to," I said, looking at my mom and Sergeant Johnson to see if it was all right with them. They nodded, and I felt relieved. I needed to leave the house for a little while, if only to have the chance to think about what had happened. It had been some afternoon. An hour ago, I'd had nothing heavier on my mind than how many miles a week I should run in order to be in shape for track tryouts — and now look. The arrival of one tiny baby had changed everything. My life had suddenly become much more complicated.

CHAPTER 3

Kristy chattered away as we drove to the meeting, telling Charlie all about the baby's mysterious appearance on my doorstep. I heard her talking, but I wasn't paying much attention. I couldn't stop thinking about the baby — how cute he was, and how mysterious and exciting it was that he had turned up at my house. Exciting and worrisome. How were we going to track down his parents?

I couldn't wait to tell my BSC friends about the baby. I knew they'd be just as excited as I was. After all, babies don't turn up on doorsteps every day.

I looked at Kristy and couldn't help grinning as I remembered how she'd jumped into action when she heard about the baby's arrival. Ms. Take Charge, that's Kristy for you. I guess everyone has his or her own way of reacting to unusual circumstances. I thought about each of my friends in the BSC and tried to predict what each would do if a baby appeared on her doorstep.

Kristy, as you've already seen, never wastes time trying to decide what to do; she just does it. She's a natural-born leader, full of good ideas and blessed with the energy and drive to bring those ideas to life.

The BSC owes its existence to Kristy. She's the one who had the idea for the club. She figured out that it would be great to have one phone number at which parents could reach a whole bunch of experienced sitters, instead of having to make a zillion calls every time they needed someone to watch their kids. Like most of Kristy's ideas, this one was very simple, and yet it was brilliant. At first the club advertised with fliers and newspaper ads, but now we hardly ever need to do that. Satisfied parents are the only advertising we need. We meet every Monday, Wednesday, and Friday afternoon from 5:30 to 6:00, and we usually receive plenty of calls.

Kristy wasn't content with a thriving business, though. She had to keep making it better. So she came up with some more ideas. The club notebook, for example, in which we each write notes about every job we go on. (Parents love the fact that we're up-to-date with what's happening with our charges.) And the record book, in which we keep track of schedules and client information. And Kid-Kits. Kid-Kits are a huge hit with our charges. They're cardboard boxes we've decorated and then filled with stickers, markers, and hand-me-down toys and books that are new and exciting to the kids we sit for. We don't take them on every job, but Kid-Kits are a BSC trademark.

Anyway, back to Kristy. She has long brown hair and brown eyes, and she's on the short side. She's not into fashion or makeup. She dresses in jeans and a turtleneck just about every day. She says she's too busy to bother with dressing up, and I guess she is. Besides running the BSC, she coaches a softball team, Kristy's Krushers. (I'm proud to be their assistant coach.) Also, she has a huge family, so her house is majorly chaotic. Kristy has two older brothers, Charlie (our driver, age seventeen) and Sam (who's fifteen), plus one younger one, David Michael (age seven). That's the family she grew up with: her brothers and her mother. Her dad cut out on them way back when David Michael was a baby.

But Kristy's family has changed — and grown — a lot in the recent past. It all started when Kristy's mom fell in love with a man named Watson Brewer, who happens to be mega-rich. Wedding bells rang, and Kristy and her brothers moved across town to live in Watson's mansion (which happens to be two houses down from mine). Watson has two children from his first marriage, Karen and Andrew, who live at the mansion part-time. And then, soon after their marriage, Watson and Kristy's mom decided to adopt a baby, so Emily Michelle came to live at the mansion, too. She's an incredibly cute two-and-a-half-year-old who was born in Vietnam. Soon after *she* arrived, Nannie came to help out with everything. Full house, right? And that's not even counting the puppy (Shannon), the cat (Boo-Boo), the goldfish, the hermit crab, and the rat. (What a menagerie! I'd be sneezing my head off if I lived there.)

Anyway, you can see why Kristy wasn't fazed by a baby showing up on my doorstep.

Next, I thought about Claudia Kishi. We were on our way to her house, since the BSC meetings are held in Claudia's room. Why? Because she has her own phone, with a private line. That's how she ended up being named vice-president. You know how the vice-president of the country doesn't seem to have many actual responsibilities? Well, that's true of the VP of the BSC, too. The only thing Claud really has to do is answer the phone (and take care of any BSC business that comes up) during nonmeeting times. However, she's also taken it upon herself to be the OSMP: Official Snack and Munchie Provider. But that's a labor of love. Claud's a junk-food junkie.

I wondered how Claud would react to finding a baby on her doorstep. If her reaction to the birth of her cousin and godchild, Lynn, was any indication, Claudia would be thrilled. She might even go a little overboard, the way she did after Lynn was born. She bought the baby so many presents and spent so much time "helping" the baby's parents that she succeeded in making a major pest of herself.

She's probably learned from that experience, but I bet she'd dive right into making the baby a gorgeous mobile, or start painting a mural for the room it'd be staying in. See, Claudia's an artist — a very talented one. I've never met anyone who can out-draw, out-paint, out-sculpt, or out-*create* Claudia. Even her way of dressing is creative. Her outfits are never boring, that's for sure.

Claudia's not an academic genius, like her older sister, Janine (who takes college courses, even though she's only sixteen). In fact, Claudia has so much trouble in school that she was recently sent back to seventh grade. (Until then, she was in eighth, like most of the rest of the BSC members.) After a difficult adjustment period, she's actually doing well, and I think it's a real treat for her to be making A's and B's for a change.

Claudia is Japanese-American and truly

beautiful, with long black hair that she's always fixing in new and interesting ways; dark, almond-shaped eyes; and a figure to die for, even though she practically lives on Doritos. (Her parents detest her junk food habit and also disapprove of her love of Nancy Drew mysteries. But Claud refuses to give them up.)

Claudia's best friend, and the BSC's treasurer, is Stacey McGill. Stacey is a savvy, sassy, sophisticated sort. (That's called alliteration — when all the words start with the same letter. We learned about it in English the other day.)

If Stacey found a baby on her doorstep, her first thoughts would probably be about opening a college savings account for the child, and she'd start assessing the various stock and bond options in order to figure out the most advantageous investment plan. Stacey is a whiz with numbers and enjoys math class. (As Claudia would say, "It takes all kinds.")

Stacey grew up in Manhattan, which is where her savvy, sassy sophistication comes from. She still goes there as often as possible to visit her dad. Her parents were divorced not long ago, and Stacey chose to live here in Stoneybrook with her mom, even though a big part of her heart belongs to Bloomingdale's.

Stacey has long blonde hair (usually permed into a mass of fluffy curls), blue eyes, and a knack for dressing in the trendiest styles without looking like some kind of supermodel wannabe.

Ever hear of diabetes? That's a disease in which your body doesn't process sugars correctly. Stacey has it. What that means is that she has to be very, very careful about what she eats (no sweet stuff, just a very balanced, healthy diet), and she has to monitor her blood sugar and give herself injections of insulin every day. Tough stuff, but Stacey deals with it well. I think she and I share a special understanding, since we've both had to learn to live with chronic health problems.

Mary Anne Spier, the BSC's secretary, is another person who — like Claudia — would want to make things for a baby who arrived on her doorstep. Only instead of mobiles, Mary Anne would make blankets and booties. She's a champion knitter, and it's a hobby that suits her personality. Mary Anne is a quiet, private person (so knitting makes more sense than, say, karaoke singing). She's also very warm and has a soft touch, like a knitted blanket. Mary Anne has short brown hair and brown eyes and dresses fairly conservatively (compared to Claudia, anyway).

Surprisingly, quiet Mary Anne is best friends with Hurricane Kristy. I guess it's true what they say about opposites attracting! She also has a steady boyfriend named Logan Bruno, who is a sweet-talking ex-Southerner (he's from Louisville, Kentucky), and a second best friend — and stepsister — named Dawn Schafer.

Dawn used to be in the BSC. In fact, I took her place when she moved back to California for good. (Her job — now mine — was as alternate officer, which means being on standby in case any other officer can't make it to a meeting.) Dawn's mom, a divorcée, married Mary Anne's dad (a widower ever since Mary Anne was a baby) not long ago, after Mary Anne and Dawn discovered that their parents had dated each other back in the Dark Ages, when they were in high school. Apparently, it wasn't hard to bring them back together, and then the magic happened all over again.

Now Mary Anne and her dad and Dawn's mom live in what used to be Dawn's house, an old farmhouse with a secret passage (and a ghost!), and Dawn has returned to California to live with her dad and younger brother. I know everyone in the BSC misses Dawn, Mary Anne most of all. I hardly know Dawn (I've only met her when she was home during vacations), but I can see why everybody likes her. (If *she* found a baby on her doorstep, she'd probably start reading books like *How to Raise an Organic Baby*. Dawn's seriously into health foods.)

"Almost there, Abby," Kristy called from the front seat. "Time to wake up!" She turned to grin at me. I smiled back. I hadn't said a word during the trip to Claudia's house. I was too distracted, thinking about the baby and about my friends.

There are two other members of the BSC, both of whom are a little younger than the rest of us. Their names are Mallory Pike and Jessi Ramsey, and they happen to be best friends. Mal has reddish-brown hair, glasses, and braces (which she hates), while Jessi has beautiful deep brown eyes, dark skin and the long, long legs of a dancer. They're both eleven and in sixth grade, and are excellent, responsible sitters. Since they're younger, their parents don't allow them to sit nights (unless it's for their own siblings), so they end up taking a lot of afternoon jobs.

Let's see, what would Mal do if she found a baby on her doorstep? Well, first of all, she probably wouldn't freak out. Mal's used to babies and kids, since she has seven — count 'em, *seven* — younger sisters and brothers. No, she wouldn't panic. Instead, she'd probably start thinking about all the picture books she'd write and illustrate for the baby. Mal loves to write and draw and she wants to be a children's author some day.

Jessi's reaction to a baby? She'd probably

measure its little feet and order its first ballet slippers. Jessi's a dance fanatic who takes classes and practices regularly (she wakes up at, like, 5:00 A.M. in order to work out). She's very talented. Her family's smaller than Mal's. She has a younger sister and a baby brother, plus an aunt who lives with the family.

So that's the BSC. Don't they sound like a great group? I feel so lucky to have been invited to join the club. (Anna was invited, also, but she's too busy with her music.)

Oh, I almost forgot. There are two associate members of the BSC who help out if we're overbooked. One of them is Logan Bruno, Mary Anne's beau. The other is Shannon Kilbourne, who lives near Kristy and me but goes to private school. I don't know either of them all that well, since they don't usually come to meetings, but they seem very nice.

"Yo, Abby!" Kristy's voice interrupted my thoughts. "We're here!" She was climbing out of the car. Somehow we'd arrived at Claudia's without my even realizing it, and it was time for our meeting to begin.

CHAPTER 4

I followed Kristy as she let herself in (the Kishis' front door is never locked when it's BSC meeting time) and pounded up the stairs.

"Ahem!" said Claudia, when we walked into her room. She looked at her digital clock, and then at Kristy. Then she raised her eyebrows.

Claudia was sitting cross-legged on her bed, sorting through a pile of Hershey's Miniatures. I knew she was looking for all the Special Dark bars, since those are her favorites. She was wearing a typical Claudia outfit: a funky red-flannel minidress layered with a black-and-white-checked thrift-shop man's vest, black tights, and red high-tops. Her hair was in this sort of sideways ponytail (that's the only way I can describe it), held by a red scrunchie.

Next to her on the bed was Stacey, who was polishing a green Granny Smith apple on her jeans. Of course, since this is Stacey we're talking about, they weren't just regular jeans. They were stonewashed to a perfect degree of faded blue, and torn at the knee in this casual-yet-not-sloppy way. She wore them with a crisp white shirt, a green V-necked sweater, and brown Hush Puppies, and she looked like something out of a magazine ad.

Next to Stacey was Mary Anne, who was peeling the wrapper off a miniature Mr. Goodbar that Claudia must have given her. She smiled a warm greeting as we walked in. Nobody has made me feel more welcome in the BSC than Mary Anne. She just has this way about her that makes you feel instantly at home.

Jessi and Mal were sprawled in their favorite spots on the floor. Mal was writing in the BSC notebook. Unlike the rest of us, who think it's kind of a pain to write up all our jobs — even though we know it's a good idea — Mal absolutely loves to record her thoughts and impressions in the notebook. Her entries make great reading, too. She knows how to make even the most boring sitting job sound fascinating.

Jessi, who never wastes an opportunity to stretch those hard-working muscles of hers, was sitting with her legs spread out and had bent over between them. She is so limber! I mean, her elbows and forearms were on the floor, if you can picture it. I'll never be able to do that, even though I stretch every day. Jessi is like Gumby.

Everybody looked up when Claudia cleared her throat. "Ahem," she said again, grinning at Kristy as she pointed at the clock.

One thing you have to know about Kristy is that she is an absolute *bear* on the topic of punctuality. She believes not only that you should always be on time, but that you should strive to be five or ten minutes early. Which is why it's a very, very rare thing for Kristy to walk into Claudia's room and find all the other members of the BSC already on hand. Usually it's Kristy making those throat-clearing noises and looking at the clock.

Kristy's face was bright red. Was it from the excitement of what she and I had just been through? Was it because she had just broken the world record for the up-the-stairs dash? Or maybe, just maybe, was it because she was majorly embarrassed because everyone else had beaten her to the meeting?

I think it was a combination of all three.

In any case, it wasn't as if we were actually late. Just as Kristy began to walk toward her usual spot in the director's chair by Claudia's desk, the numbers on the clock flipped over to 5:30. "I hereby call this meeting to order," Kristy said in a rush, as she plopped down and stuck a pencil over her ear. Then, without pausing, she blurted out, "You guys will never believe what just happened!"

Normally, Kristy is pretty strict about what we discuss at the beginning of meetings. If it's not club business, she'll cut you off and tell you to wait until all the club business has been discussed. But she's been known to break her own rule, especially if she has exciting news.

"What?" asked Stacey.

"Tell us!" said Mary Anne.

Kristy glanced over at me. "Well, actually," she said reluctantly, "it's really Abby's news. After all, the ba — I mean, it happened at her house."

I could tell it was just about killing her to hold off telling everyone about the baby. And it was killing everyone else to have to wait to find out what had happened.

"I don't care *whose* news it is. Just spill it!" begged Claudia, leaning forward and letting her handful of carefully selected Miniatures fall back into the pile.

"Well," I began. "You'll never guess what I found on the porch when I came home from school today." I paused and looked around, but nobody seemed to want to waste time guessing.

"I'll give you a hint," said Kristy. "What's little and smells sweet and makes you smile?"

She was practically jumping out of her seat.

"Flowers?" asked Stacey.

"A Hershey's Kiss?" guessed Claudia.

"A kitten?" asked Mary Anne.

"Mary Anne's the closest," I said. "Since a kitten is a baby cat. But what I found was a baby. A human one. A boy."

"No way!" yelled Claudia.

"A baby on your doorstep?" asked Mal. "You must be kidding." I saw her and Jessi exchange a wide-eyed glance.

"I'm not," I said, crossing my heart and holding up my palm. "It's absolutely true. Ask Kristy."

Kristy nodded. Her eyes were shining with excitement, and while she wasn't red anymore, her face was still pretty pink. "He is the cutest, sweetest, most adorable baby you've ever seen," she said.

"Where did he come from?" asked Claudia.

"What's his name?" asked Jessi.

"Why was he abandoned?" asked Stacey.

"How old is he?" asked Mary Anne.

"I don't have the answer to any of those questions," I replied. "It's a mystery. He just arrived on our doorstep. That's all I know."

The phone rang then, and I think we all remembered at the same instant that we were supposed to be having a meeting. Immediately, the club swung into official BSC mode.

"Baby-sitters Club," said Claudia, answering the phone. "Oh, hi, Mrs. Papadakis, how are you?" She listened for a moment. "Short notice is no problem," she said. "I'm sure we can find someone for tomorrow. I'll call you right back."

Mary Anne had already opened the club record book on her lap. "Tomorrow?" she asked. "What time?" When Claudia told her that Mrs. Papadakis needed a sitter for the following afternoon, it took Mary Anne just a second to check the schedule. "Actually, I'm the only one free," she said. "And I'll be glad to take the job."

Claudia called Mrs. Papadakis back, and the job was set.

As soon as Claudia finished the call, Stacey spoke up. "I hate to mention it, guys," she began, "but baby or no baby, it *is* a Monday, and you know what that means." She held up the manila envelope she uses for a treasury, and we all groaned and reached into pockets, backpacks, and purses. We like to give Stacey a hard time about paying dues, but in fact nobody really minds that much. After all, the money goes for good causes, such as paying Charlie to drive Kristy and me to meetings, covering Claudia's phone bill, and buying stickers and things for our Kid-Kits. Plus, once in awhile, if we have enough extra funds, we blow the bucks on pizza.

After we'd handed over our money, Kristy asked if there was any other club business. She's such a professional. I knew she was dying to talk about the baby, but she wasn't about to skip over anything. Anyway, Mal waved her hand.

"Jessi and I had this idea," she said. "You know how we're in this writing workshop at the library? Well, it's been a blast. It's really fun to listen to other people read their work out loud."

"We thought it might be fun for our charges to do some writing and then share it," Jessi put in. "We could declare February BSC Writing Month — "

"And then at the end of the month we could have a poetry slam!" finished Mal excitedly.

"A *what?*" asked Kristy.

"A slam," Mal repeated. "It's the latest thing. It's sort of like a talent show for writers. Everybody reads their stuff out loud, and there are prizes for the people who get the best audience response."

"Like when there's an applause meter?" asked Claudia.

"Exactly," said Mal. "Only we — the judges — will be the meter."

"Is it just for poetry?" asked Mary Anne.

"No, people can write prose, too," said Jessi. "Short stories, plays, even jokes. Anything."

"I don't think I'd be a great coach — or judge — for this," said Claudia. "I mean, I can't even spell."

"It's not about spelling," said Mal. "It's about creativity, so you'll be great. How about it, guys?"

Everybody agreed that the idea sounded like fun, and that it would be a great way to beat the February blahs.

"It's definite, then," said Kristy. "Any other business?" Nobody spoke up, so even though it wasn't six o'clock yet Kristy declared the official part of the meeting over, and we went back to discussing the baby.

I had noticed Mal and Jessi exchanging a look when I first told everyone about the baby, and now I asked about it. It turned out that there was a woman in their writing group who had just written — and read out loud — a story about a mother abandoning her baby. Apparently, the same idea had struck them both: Could she be the one who had left the car seat on my porch?

"I mean, I know it's a mistake to confuse fiction with fact," said Mal.

"But I think we should keep an eye on her anyway," added Jessi.

We all agreed that that would be a good idea and made plans to follow up any other leads that might help us solve this new mystery that had landed on my doorstep.

I started my own investigation that very night. When I arrived home, my mom announced that we'd be keeping the baby. "Just until his mother is found," she said.

"Is that really okay?" I asked. "I thought he'd have to go to child welfare or something."

"We've cleared it with the authorities," my mom said. "They all agree that this is the best place for the baby, at least for now." She looked away when she said that, and I had the feeling there was something she knew and wasn't telling me. I was about to ask her some more questions, but the baby chose that moment to start crying, and soon we were rushing around trying to figure out what he needed.

Later, as I sat in my room trying to do my homework, I realized that there was no way I could concentrate. I was dying to know where the baby had come from, and I had a feeling I wouldn't be able to focus on anything else until the mystery was solved.

I stepped out into the hall and listened. I heard my mother moving around in her study and knew she must be trying to catch up on some of the work she'd missed that day. From Anna's room came the sound of scales. As usual, she was using the last hour before bedtime to practice her violin. I didn't hear the baby. He must have been asleep in my mom's room, in the crib we'd borrowed from Watson, who'd stored Emily Michelle's in his attic.

I tiptoed downstairs and grabbed a flashlight and my jacket from the hall closet. Then I slipped outside and began to search methodically, up and down the walk, all over the porch, and back and forth across the driveway. What was I looking for? Anything. Anything that might give me a clue about the baby's identity. Maybe I'd missed a note, or perhaps I would find a dropped glove or some footprints.

Finally, just as I was about to give up, I found something near the end of the driveway. It was a receipt — from a drugstore in New York City. Who had dropped it? It could have been my mom, but it also could have been the person who left the baby. It wasn't much of a clue, but it was better than nothing. I stuck it into my pocket and headed toward the house.

Just then, I heard the faint sound of crying. I looked up in time to see the light go on in my mom's bedroom. I watched from outside as she walked into the room, picked up the baby, and strolled around with him cradled in her arms, trying to comfort him. His cries grew louder at first, but finally he began to settle down.

The poor kid. Did he feel rejected? How could anybody abandon such an adorable boy? I resolved then and there that I wouldn't stop investigating until I knew the whole truth about the baby — who he belonged to, why they had given him up. It was the least I could do for the vulnerable little stranger who had turned up at my house.

CHAPTER 5

Tuesday

Well, BSC Writing Month is off to a good start. The kids just love it. And, with Eli around for inspiration, they're creating some great literature.

That's Mary Anne, writing up her job at the Papadakises' in the club notebook. Only she and her charges didn't spend much of that afternoon at the Papadakis house. They, along with just about everybody else in the neighborhood, came to our house. They didn't come to see me or Anna, either. They came to see Eli.

Who's Eli? Take a guess. That's the name we gave our mystery baby. After all, if he was going to be staying with us for awhile, he had to have a name. We couldn't just refer to him as "the baby" forever, could we?

On Eli's second day with us, my mom stayed home from work again. The heating system was still down at her office, and besides, someone had to stay with Eli while Anna and I were at school.

Speaking of school, I almost didn't make it there that day. Being around Eli was so much more fun than sitting in social studies class. Who would want to trade a happy, gurgling baby for a dull, droning teacher?

That morning I woke up early. Well, actually, I was *woken* up. By Eli. But I couldn't blame him. If you can't talk, how else are you going to let people know that you're hungry and your diaper is wet and you want to come out of your crib? Crying makes a lot of sense under those circumstances, don't you think?

Eli's cries brought results, too. Within minutes, he had three handmaidens waiting on him. I changed his diaper while Anna dug around in the blue diaper bag for a clean sleeper. Meanwhile, my mom headed downstairs to warm some formula. Soon, I had a happy, dry, clean baby sitting on my lap, sucking contentedly on a bottle. Again, I leaned down to sniff the top of his head. Mmmm! There's no smell that can compare.

I stalled as long as I could — feeding Eli, burping him, putting him down for a morning nap. Eventually, though, my mom kicked Anna and me out of the house, insisting that we go to school.

I don't know what the point was. It's not as if I could concentrate at all. Instead of multiplying X and Y, I spent math class thinking about whether Eli was too young for his first baseball glove. During social studies, I gazed out the window and wondered what Eli was doing right then (not that there was much to wonder about — it was a good bet that he was either sleeping or eating, since those are the two main things that babies do). All through English class I speculated on who might have left Eli on our doorstep, and why. Mal had mentioned during our meeting that whoever had abandoned him had probably just picked our house at random because it's in a wealthy neighborhood. That sort of made sense. But why wouldn't he or she have picked an even fancier house, like Kristy's? For most of science class I thought about how cute Eli was when he smiled.

Baby love. I had it bad.

At lunchtime, my friends and I talked about Eli, and both Kristy and Mary Anne told me they wanted to stop over that afternoon to see him. It turned out that they weren't the only ones. *Everybody* wanted to visit Eli, and that's why Tuesday ended up being Open House Day at the Stevensons'.

When Mary Anne arrived at the Papadakises' that afternoon, the kids ran to her.

"Did you hear about the baby?" asked Hannie, as soon as Mary Anne walked in the door. Hannie's seven. She has dark hair and deep brown eyes and this great smile. She's best friends with Kristy's little stepsister, Karen.

"He appeared, like, out of nowhere!" Hannie's brother, Linny, added. Linny, who's nine, looks a lot like his sister. He hangs out with Kristy's little brother, David Michael, even though David Michael is two years younger.

"I heard he's really cute," said Hannie. "Can we go see him?"

Mary Anne told me later that she was a little surprised to find the Papadakis kids so excited about a baby, since they have a little sister of their own: Sari, who's two and looks like a miniature version of Hannie. "But a baby's a baby," she said. "A two-year-old just isn't the same, I guess."

True enough.

At any rate, Mary Anne was just as eager to meet Eli as the Papadakis kids were, so after a quick call to make sure it was okay with me, she brought them over.

My mother had gone out to do errands soon after Anna and I had come home from school. (Anna had — for the first time in my memory — skipped orchestra. She said she couldn't stand being away from Eli for one more *minute*.) So when Mary Anne and her charges arrived, they found Anna and me hovering over the baby, arguing happily about whose turn it would be to change his diaper next time it needed changing.

We were in the living room, and I was holding Eli (having just won a coin toss with Anna). Mary Anne and her three charges surrounded us on the couch and began cooing over the baby. (Well, Sari wasn't exactly cooing. She was more interested in banging on our piano.)

"Isn't he the sweetest thing?" cried Mary Anne, holding out her arms for him. I didn't want to hand him over, but just to be polite, I did. Mary Anne nestled her nose into the crease of his neck and breathed deeply. I guess she likes that baby smell as much as I do.

"Can I hold him?" begged Hannie.

"Let's tickle his toes and see if he laughs," suggested Linny seriously, as if the baby were a scientific experiment.

Just then the doorbell rang. "I'll answer it," I said, but nobody even looked up. Mary Anne was too busy making a face at Eli, trying to entice a smile out of him. Anna looked on as if she were a mother bear, worried about whether this strange person might hurt her cub. And Hannie and Linny were poking and prodding in a gentle, exploratory way.

I opened the door to find a small crowd on the porch. Kristy was there with David Michael, and they'd arrived at the same time as Shannon, who had given in to her younger sister Maria's begging and brought her over to see the baby. And just as I was letting that set of visitors in, another two arrived: Melody and Bill Korman, who also live in the neighborhood.

As I let them in, I looked up at our front door, half expecting to see a lighted marquee like the ones at movie theaters. "See the Mystery Baby! He Smiles, He Gurgles, He Coos! Step Right Up!"

Eli was a star.

Inside, the kids were gathered around the couch. They were talking in whispers so as not to scare Eli. "When's my turn to hold him?" asked Maria, who's eight. She hopped from foot to foot with impatience.

"You're behind me," Linny said, pushing himself closer to Mary Anne and Eli.

"Look at his little foot!" cried Melody. She's seven, and like Maria, she goes to Stoneybrook Day School instead of Stoneybrook Elementary.

Bill, Melody's nine-year-old brother, shouldered his way past her and stared at the baby. "What a little doink!" he said. He was trying to act tough, but he was just as smitten with Eli as the rest of us, even though he tried not to show it.

Eli, who had been resting peacefully, suddenly opened his eyes and looked around. He must have been shocked to see all those pairs of eyes staring back at him, because within about one half of a millisecond he screwed up his face and began to wail.

"Okay," said Mary Anne, rocking him gently. "It's okay. It's okay."

Apparently, Eli did not agree with her. He wailed more loudly.

"Maybe he needs a new diaper."

"I bet he's hungry. Where's his bottle?"

"He probably just wants a pacifier."

"I think his foot hurts him. See how he's holding it?"

All the kids were talking at once, offering ideas. They jostled each other and moved closer, prompting Eli to scream at an even higher volume.

Pandemonium.

Finally, Mary Anne couldn't take it anymore. She handed Eli to Anna, stood up, and made a T with her hands. "Hey, time out!" she called.

Somehow, her soft voice was forceful enough so that the kids heard it, even over Eli's screams and their own shouts. "The baby isn't hungry or wet or anything else. He's just confused. There's too much going on in here, and it's time for some of us to leave."

"No way!" said Hannie, folding her arms. "I didn't even hold him yet."

The other kids began to protest, too.

Mary Anne thought for a second. Then she turned to me. "Do you have a bunch of paper and pencils we could use?" she asked.

"Sure," I said, thinking of the closet in my mom's study that's always stuffed with office supplies.

"Then I think it's time to kick off BSC Writing Month," said Mary Anne. "Okay, kids, let's go. I want you all to join me in the kitchen so

48

I can tell you about a really fun activity. Then, one by one, you can take turns visiting with Eli."

The rest of the afternoon was terrific. Eli calmed down as soon as the kids dispersed, and he seemed to enjoy visiting with them one at a time. In the kitchen, Mary Anne told the kids about BSC Writing Month and about the different types of writing they could do. "You can write poems or stories or even songs," she said. "Anything you want. And you can write about any subject in the world: flowers or puppies or sunsets or dinosaurs or worms."

Mary Anne must have been inspiring. That day, the kids wrote and wrote. But can you guess what topic every single kid ended up writing about?

Right. Baby Eli.

CHAPTER 6

"Hello, Abby. How's that baby? Taking good care of him?"

Later that evening, I'd answered a knock on the door to find Sergeant Johnson and a woman I didn't know standing on the porch. I'd been sitting in the living room, keeping an eye on Eli while I worked on my social studies homework. Anna was upstairs practicing — I could hear the faint sounds of her scales — and my mom was in her study. The house felt very peaceful after the chaos of that afternoon.

"He's great," I told Sergeant Johnson. My voice was shaking a little, but I don't think he or the woman noticed. Was this Eli's mother? I felt the weirdest mix of happiness and sadness. Happiness that Eli and his mom would be reunited, and sadness at the thought of seeing him leave our house. "I think he recognizes my voice already." I invited them inside.

"This is Ms. Stapleton," said Sergeant Johnson, gesturing toward the woman, who was almost as tall as he was, with blonde hair and a no-nonsense look on her face. "She's from social services."

"Oh," I said, my face falling. I felt this strange sense of relief that she wasn't Eli's mom, but then a new concern sprang to mind. Had they come to take Eli away? I felt tears spring to my eyes, which surprised me. Hoping that neither of my visitors had noticed, I blinked them away.

"We're just here to check up on the baby and make sure everything's all right," said Ms. Stapleton in a warm voice. She sounded a lot nicer than she looked.

"Oh!" I said, relieved. "Well, he's sleeping right now, but I'm sure we won't wake him if we tiptoe in and take a look. He's in the living room." I suddenly realized that Ms. Stapleton might not approve of our allowing Eli to sleep on the couch. "He has his own crib," I added hastily. "Upstairs, in my mom's room. But he fell asleep on the couch, and Anna and I thought it was better not to wake him up just to put him to bed, if you know what I mean."

Sergeant Johnson gave me a kind smile. "Lead the way," he said.

I brought them into the living room and showed them where Eli was sleeping. "We arranged all the pillows around him so he couldn't possibly roll off the couch," I whispered, still concerned that Ms. Stapleton would think I didn't know how to take care of a baby.

"Shhh!" she said, pointing to Eli, who was moving his arms as if he were about to wake up. "I see. He looks perfectly safe and very, very comfortable." She was whispering, too.

Then the three of us just stood there gazing at him for a few moments as he heaved a sigh and settled back into a deep sleep. I could tell by glancing at her face that Ms. Stapleton was charmed by Eli, just as everyone else had been.

"Shall we?" asked Sergeant Johnson, gesturing toward the kitchen.

We tiptoed out of the living room and gathered in the kitchen. "Would you like some coffee?" I asked. "Tea? Formula?" I held up a can of Eli's formula and grinned. I wasn't worried anymore about Ms. Stapleton. She hadn't come to take Eli away. She'd just come to make sure he was all right.

"I'd love some coffee," said Ms. Stapleton.

"So would I," said Sergeant Johnson. "I'm on duty until midnight."

I bustled around, setting out the coffee-maker, two mugs, cream, and sugar.

"Your mother said she'd be home tonight," said Sergeant Johnson.

"Oh, she is!" I assured him. "She's just busy working. She probably didn't even hear you come in. Should I tell her you're here?"

"If you would," said Sergeant Johnson. "We have a few things to discuss with her."

That sounded serious. As soon as I'd turned on the coffeemaker, I ran to find my mom. She turned off her computer when she heard who was there and followed me downstairs. I poured the coffee and put some cookies on a plate for our guests. Then I started to sit down at the table.

"Uh, Abby," began Sergeant Johnson. "If you'll excuse us, we'd like to talk to your mom in private."

"In private?" I repeated. Then I realized that he wanted me to leave. "Oh, sure. Okay. I'll just — I'll just be with Eli." I stood up and backed out of the room. Darn! What could they possibly have to talk about that they couldn't share with me? It must be something about Eli, and where he came from. I had been heading to the living room, but suddenly I stopped and looked back at the closed kitchen door.

I knew it was wrong, but I just couldn't resist. I tiptoed toward the kitchen and slowly, quietly, I knelt by the closed door and listened. I could hear voices, but I couldn't make out what they were saying. I put my ear up to the door and listened harder.

"What are you doing?"

I nearly jumped out of my skin when I heard Anna's voice behind me.

"Nothing! Nothing," I said. Quickly, I moved away from the door.

Anna frowned at me. "You weren't eavesdropping, were you?"

"Who me?" I asked. "No way. Not me. Uh-uh."

Anna looked skeptical.

"Well, maybe a little. But they're talking about Eli, and I need to know what they're saying. Maybe they've figured out who left him."

We were in the living room now. Anna looked at Eli and smiled. "He's such a doll," she said. "What does it matter where he came from? He's here now. Let's enjoy him while he's with us."

Just then, Eli stirred, stretched, opened his eyes, and started to wail. Both of us sprang into action. Anna picked him up. "He's wet," she said.

"Let's take him upstairs, as long as he's

awake. We can change him and put him back to sleep in his crib," I said.

Which is exactly what we did. Soon Eli was sleeping peacefully again, while we stood over his crib, gazing at him. Then the phone rang, and I ran to grab it before it woke him up.

It was Mal. "How's Eli?" she asked.

I told her he was perfect.

"I just wanted to let you know that Jessi and I are going to check out that woman from our writing group. She did something very suspicious tonight."

"What?" I asked.

"She didn't show up for our meeting," said Mal. "Don't you think that means something? Anyway, Jessi and I asked a few questions and we think we found out where she lives. We're going to try to follow her and figure out what she's up to."

"Great," I said. I wasn't convinced that this was a lead, but it couldn't hurt for Mal and Jessi to check this woman out. Probably the woman's story was just that: a story. Still, you never know.

Thinking of stories reminded me of the stories and poems the kids had written that afternoon. I decided that this was a good time to read them. Maybe they would take my mind off the mystery, and off the frustration of not being able to listen in on the meeting going on downstairs.

After a brief search, I found the pile of papers in the living room. I brought them upstairs and made myself comfortable on my bed. Then I began to read.

The first story I picked up was by David Michael:

THERE WAS ONCE A BABY NAMED ELI, WHO HAD BROWN HAIR AND BLUE EYES. WHEN HE GREW UP HE BECAME A PRINCE AND FOUGHT A BUNCH OF DRAGONS. HE WAS THE BRAVEST PRINCE IN THE WORLD.

Then there was a great poem by Melody Korman:

Babies are happy,
babies are cute,
Babies have tiny feet that
won't fit in my boot.
I love babies except
when they cry
And that's why I love
baby Eli.

Linny had written a story about a space alien that had taken the form of a baby, and

Bill Korman had illustrated it (he'd said he didn't feel like writing that day). And Hannie had written a song called "Eli, the Best Baby in the Universe."

But it was Maria Kilbourne's story that caught my interest.

Once upon a time, a baby came to the sleepy little town of Stoneybrook. It was the cutest baby anybody had ever seen. It arrived one afternoon in a green car. The people who found it loved it very much and —

Green car? I stopped reading. Where had that come from?

I threw down the paper, flew to the phone, and dialed with trembling fingers. "Shannon? Hi, it's Abby." I started babbling, telling her what I'd just read. "Is Maria there? I want to ask her about this story."

"She already went to bed," said Shannon. "But I'll go wake her up. This sounds important."

"No, don't wake her — " I began, but it was too late. Shannon had already put down the phone.

"Hello?"

Maria sounded groggy, but she answered

my questions anyway. She'd been home sick the day before, and it turned out that she had, indeed, seen somebody climb out of a green car and drop something off at my house. No, she hadn't been able to tell what it was. No, she didn't get a good look at the person — though she thought the person had been short and might have been a woman. And no, she hadn't looked at the license plate.

Maria said she didn't think anything of it at the time, but when she heard about Eli arriving she'd decided to make up a fairy tale about how he'd come, and she'd used the green car as part of her story. That was all.

I thanked her and told her to go right back to bed. Then I said a quick good-bye to Shannon and ran downstairs. Private meeting or not, I had to interrupt, to tell Sergeant Johnson what I'd learned. It might add up to nothing, but on the other hand, it might be an important lead.

I reached up to knock on the kitchen door, and just then, the doorbell rang.

CHAPTER 7

I stopped in my tracks and glanced at my watch. It was after nine. Who could be ringing our bell? A little shiver ran down my spine, and somehow I just *knew* that the person at the door had something to do with Eli.

I was right, sort of.

"I'll answer that," I called out, even though nobody else was in sight. I went to the door and flicked on the inside hall light as well as the outdoor light, the one that illuminates the porch. Then, following the official standard baby-sitter precaution (since it was nighttime and I wasn't expecting anyone), I peeked through the peephole.

What — or who — was I expecting to see? Another police officer? An FBI agent? Eli's mother? A kidnapper? A blackmailer?

I guess I was expecting anyone *but* the person I saw standing on our porch. She stood waiting for the door to open, and she looked very anxious. She was a slightly built, mousy-looking woman with limp dark blonde hair and tiny hands, which she wrung nervously. She wore a tweed overcoat that looked about three sizes too big and carried a large brown leather bag, too big to be a pocketbook but too small to be a suitcase.

She looked a little like a child dressed up in her mother's clothes.

"Who is it?"

I jumped back, surprised. My mom, who must have heard the bell ring, had appeared behind me.

"I have no idea," I said. I looked through the peephole one more time, then stepped back to let my mother see.

She looked, shrugged (she didn't seem to recognize the woman either), and opened the door.

"You requested a nanny?" asked the woman in a thin, reedy voice. She gulped loudly enough so I could hear. "This *is* the Stevensons', isn't it?" she asked timidly.

"It is," said my mother. "And I did. Request a nanny, that is. But I certainly didn't expect anyone so soon." She looked a little perplexed. "The agency told me it might take until Friday."

"I wanted to come as soon as I could," the woman said. She pulled a messy sheaf of papers out of the large pocket in her coat. "Here are my references," she added, shoving them at my mom.

"Why don't you come in?" said my mother gently. I could tell she was trying to put the woman at ease.

The woman stepped into the front hall and stopped to look around. "You have a lovely home," she said shyly. She put down her bag, and my mother eyed it.

"Uh, I'm not sure if your agency told you, but this isn't a sleep-in job," she said.

The woman blushed. Obviously, she'd thought it was, which was why she'd brought her overnight bag.

"I'm Rachel Stevenson, and this is my daughter Abby," said my mom, rushing in to ease the situation again. "Abby has a twin sister, Anna, who's upstairs right now."

"I'm Erin Amesely," said the woman. She stuck out her hand hesitantly, as if she weren't sure if it was the right thing to do. First my mother shook it, then I did.

"Pleased to meet you," I said, even though I wasn't sure that was true. This woman made me feel very suspicious. She certainly did not seem like your basic, ordinary nanny. And she wasn't a fun nanny, either. She wasn't anything like Julie Andrews as Mary Poppins.

Who was she? Did she have some motive

for being near Eli? I stared at her while my mother, who didn't seem to notice her weird behavior, filled her in on Eli.

"He's four months old," she said, as if she knew that for a fact. I realized that she wasn't telling Erin Amesely the whole story. Instead, she was acting as if Eli were just part of our family. "He's a very easy baby — not colicky or anything like that. We'd just need you here to watch him during the day, while I'm at work and the girls are at school."

Erin was nodding. "Babies that age are wonderful, aren't they?" she said softly. "I have a nephew — " she began, but then she noticed that my mother had started to glance through her references, and she clammed up and began to bite her lip nervously.

After a few moments, my mom looked up and smiled. "These references look fine," she said. "I think you can consider the job yours. Can you be here by seven tomorrow morning?"

"Oh, yes," said Erin. "Seven o'clock sharp. No problem. Thank you. Thank you very much." She looked eager.

When my mom began to talk about wages and benefits, I excused myself and headed upstairs. Just hearing my mom talk about Eli had made me want to see him and hold him. I tiptoed as I walked into my mom's room, but when I got closer to the crib I found out that tiptoeing hadn't been necessary. Eli was awake.

He lay there, looking up at me with those innocent, trusting blue eyes. "Oh, you are the sweetest boy," I said softly, as I scooped him up into my arms. I kissed the top of his head, and then his nose, and then his dimpled chin. He yawned, stretched his little arms, and gave me one of those special smiles of his.

I never knew I could fall in love so quickly.

I waltzed around the room with him, singing softly as I dipped and whirled. "You are my sunshine, my only sunshine," I sang, "you make me happy, when skies are gray." Eli gurgled and smiled up at me, and I knew he didn't care about the fact that I can't carry a tune to save my life.

"I hope Ms. Erin Amesely knows how to take good care of you," I whispered to him. "I hope she understands your baby language as well as I do." I wasn't happy about having to leave Eli with a stranger, especially with such a *strange* stranger — but what could I do? My mom was the one who would be paying for the nanny, and if she thought Erin was okay, that was that. I knew I had no say in the matter.

"Abby?"

I turned to see my mother standing in the

doorway. She had a peculiar expression on her face. "Abby, your grandparents are on the phone. They'd like to say hello to you."

I'd been so involved with Eli that I hadn't even heard the phone ring.

"I've already told them about the baby," said my mom, holding out her arms for Eli. "But why don't you go ahead and talk with them a little?"

I handed Eli over. Then I left the room and picked up the hall phone. "Hello?" I said. "Grandpa Morris? Gram Elsie?" I knew they'd both be on the phone. They always use both extensions when they call.

"Who else, bubbelah?" That was Gram Elsie. "Bubbelah" is a Yiddish word with several meanings. My grandmother uses it as a pet name for me, like "sweetie," or "darling."

"How's our Avigail?" asked Grandpa Morris, using my Hebrew name.

"I'm fine," I answered. "Did you hear about the baby?" I knew they had, but I sort of wanted to tell them about him all over again.

"Sure, honey, we heard," said Grandpa Morris. "Now, tell us how you're doing in school."

"Okay," I said. "I had a math test yesterday, and I only made two mistakes on it."

"Mazel tov!" said Gram Elsie. Another Yiddish phrase. It's used to say "congratulations."

"Thanks," I said. "So, did mom tell you how

cute Eli is?" I asked. Somehow, I was beginning to sense that they didn't want to talk about the baby — what *had* my mother told them, exactly? — but I wanted to make sure I was right.

"Cute, sure," said Grandpa Morris. "But nobody could be as cute as our Abby."

They were avoiding the topic. "So, what's new with you?" I asked. Maybe, just maybe, they'd let something slip so I'd know exactly what my mom had told them.

"My garden club is hosting this year's Spring Ball," Gram Elsie told me. "And guess who's president of the decorations committee?"

"My lovely bride, that's who," chimed in Grandpa Morris. "How do you like that?"

"That's wonderful," I said. I chatted with them for a few more minutes, as they told me all the details of their life down in Florida. Then I hung up, feeling unsatisfied. I always love talking to my grandparents, but this time something felt "off" about the conversation. Why didn't they want to talk about Eli? I stood there, staring at the phone for a few seconds. Then I shrugged and went back into my mom's room to see how Eli was doing.

"Ssshhh!" said my mom, as I walked in. She was just lowering a sleeping Eli into his crib. "Nighty night," she whispered to him, as she pulled the blanket up to his shoulders. I stood next to her, gazing down at him. When I looked back at her, I saw that she was wearing that peculiar expression again.

"Don't get too attached, sweetie," she whispered, putting a hand on my shoulder. "One of these days his mother will probably be back to take him away."

I nodded, knowing it was already far too late for me to avoid becoming attached to Eli. I bent down and kissed him good night softly, so as not to wake him. Then I kissed my mom, too, and headed off to bed.

As I lay there waiting for sleep to come, I thought about the mystery of Eli's appearance. Would I ever learn the truth? And what did my mother know that she wasn't telling me? She can be so closemouthed when she wants to be. There's no point in trying to make her talk when she prefers not to.

Just before I fell asleep, I thought of something. Why had my mom talked about the baby's *mother* coming, rather than his parents, or his father? That was the second time she'd said something like that. And why had she said "probably"? If I remembered, I'd ask her in the morning. And if I pushed her, she'd *have* to tell me what she knew. If I could convince her to talk to me, maybe I'd find some answers to my questions.

CHAPTER 8

Tuesday

Leave it to my brothers and sisters. Who else could take a writing workshop and turn it into a three ring circus? Oh, well, at least they all ended up having fun.

Right! And fun is the whole point isn't it?

Definitely. Believe it: These kids will never see poetry as boring. And I think some of those poems the triplets wrote may go down in history . . . .

It took Jessi and Mal quite a while to write up the events of that Tuesday afternoon (a week and a day A.E. — After Eli) in the club notebook. It had been a long, long day.

Mal was sitting for her sisters and brothers that day (the Pikes used to require two sitters, but now, as long as one of the triplets is around, one is enough), and Jessi was sitting for her sister, Becca. The two of them had decided to bring the kids together for a writing workshop at the Pikes'. It was a dreary, gray afternoon, and they figured it would be a quiet, peaceful way to pass the time and keep the kids occupied.

Ha!

They should have known better. After all, Mal *lives* with her siblings, and Jessi's sat for them often enough. No day inside with the Pikes can ever be quiet and peaceful, no matter what activity you've planned.

Things were already close to out of control by the time Jessi and Becca arrived. Vanessa greeted them at the door.

"Hi, come on in," she said glumly.

Jessi could tell that something must be very, very wrong. Why? Because Vanessa wasn't talking in rhyme. She's nine and wants desperately to be a poet when she grows up. Normally, she'd answer the door saying something like, "Welcome to our house, my friend. I hope this day will never end!"

Becca skipped away to find the other kids, but Jessi stayed with Vanessa. "What's the matter?" she asked.

"Nothing," said Vanessa with a big sniff.

"Come on, you can tell me," said Jessi, leading her to the stairs. They sat down together, and Jessi put an arm around Vanessa's shoulders. "What is it?" she asked.

"It's — it's — " began Vanessa, but she was interrupted by a series of loud shrieks that came closer and closer.

"Make him stop! Make him stop!" That was Margo, who's seven. She was running along with her hands over her ears, trying not to hear the words her brother Byron was shouting as he chased after her.

"Snot is gluey and snot is green, snot is the coolest thing I've ever seen," he chanted. Byron, who's ten, is one of the Pike triplets.

"Eww!" said Jessi. "That's disgusting."

"No it isn't," Byron said, skidding to a halt. "It's poetry. Mal says poetry can be about anything." He gave Jessi a devilish grin.

Just then, the other two triplets came running into the hall. "Byron, listen to this one!" shouted Adam, who was laughing so hard that his face had turned bright red.

"When your stomach feels all funny, if

you've eaten too much honey, all you have to do is puke, puke, puke!" began Jordan, who was also laughing and could barely get the words out. "When you're urpy, when you're burpy, all you have to do is — "

"Please, stop them!" begged Margo. "Or else I'll — " She looked a little green.

Mal, who had followed the triplets into the hall, spoke up. She's well acquainted with the fact that Margo has a weak stomach, and she knew it was no joke. "That's enough, guys," she said. "You can go on writing poems about anything you want, but don't force them on someone who doesn't want to listen."

"But — " began Jordan.

Margo turned toward him and puffed out her cheeks a little. He backpedaled quickly out of her way. "Let's go, guys," he said. "We can concentrate better on our writing if we do it up in our room."

The three of them ran off, giggling like hyenas. Mal and Jessi looked at each other and shook their heads. "What can you do?" Mal asked, shrugging. "It's not as if I really expected them to write poems about love or the beauty of nature."

"Why do they have to write poems at all?" wailed Vanessa. "*I'm* the poet in the family. They don't even know how to make good rhymes!"

70

"Vanessa," Jessi said gently. "All poetry doesn't have to — "

"What do you know?" interrupted Vanessa, standing up. "I'm going up to my room. I hate you all!" She stomped up the stairs, and a few seconds later Mal and Jessi heard a door slam.

"So far, so good," said Mal, smiling. "Now, how are you doing, Margo? Feeling better?" She bent down to smooth back her little sister's hair.

"Uh-huh," said Margo. "I guess so."

"Then why don't you go find Nicky and Claire and Becca," suggested Mal, "and see how they're doing with their writing." She gave Margo a little push in the right direction — toward the rec room — and then turned to Jessi.

"What do you think we should do about Vanessa?" she asked. "I can see why she might be upset. After all, it's as if everybody's trespassing on her territory. Up until now, she *has* been the poet in the family."

"I don't know," said Jessi. "How about if we leave her alone for a little while, and we'll think about it. I bet she's up there composing a poem about how awful her family is. Let's give her a chance to settle down a bit."

"Okay," said Mal. "Meanwhile, let's go see what the others are up to."

The two of them headed for the rec room,

where they found Nicky, Margo, Becca, and Claire seated around the table the Pike kids usually use for art projects. The three older kids — Nicky (he's eight), Becca (also eight), and Margo were just sitting there, looking bored, while Claire, tongue between her lips in concentration, printed careful letters with a crayon. Claire's five and is just beginning to read and write.

"How do you spell 'the'?" she asked.

Nicky rolled his eyes. "T-H-E," he answered impatiently. "This is ridiculous," he added in a lower voice.

Claire didn't seem to hear him. Mal told me later that she was concentrating so hard on making her letters correctly that she probably wouldn't have heard a fire truck if it drove through the rec room.

She finished writing and sighed contentedly. Then she frowned. "How do you spell 'mouse'?" she asked.

"Just finish your part and pass it along!" said Nicky. "Everybody's waiting for their turn." He gave an exasperated sigh.

Claire sniffed. "But I'm not done yet," she said. "No fair!"

Mal sensed a tantrum in the making. "What are you guys doing, anyway?" she asked quickly.

"We're writing a story together," said Becca.

"It's one of the activities from that book you showed us," said Margo, pointing to a book about teaching kids how to write that Mal had brought home from the library.

"Each of us writes a sentence or two, and then we pass it along. It's really fun," said Margo.

"It *could* be fun," Nicky said, glaring at Claire. "If certain people didn't take so long to write their dumb little sentences."

"Nicky!" Mal said. "That's mean."

Claire burst into tears. "My sen-sentences are just as good as yours!" she cried, rushing into Mal's arms.

"Nicky, why don't you read us what you guys have written so far?" asked Jessi, hoping to defuse the situation. "It sounds like a neat idea."

Nicky grabbed the piece of paper Claire had been working on. "I went first," he said. "Here's what I wrote: 'Once upon a time, there was a strong, brave prince named Nicky. Only he didn't know he was a prince. He thought he was just a regular boy.'"

"Great start," said Mal.

"Then Margo went," continued Nicky. "Here's her part. 'The prince had a beautiful sister, too. Her name was Margo, and she didn't know she was a princess.'"

Margo smiled happily.

"Then Becca wrote this part," said Nicky. "'One day, Nicky and Margo decided to go for a picnic in the woods near their house. Little did they know that there was a dragon roaming in those very same woods.'"

"Excellent!" said Jessi.

"Yeah, but now listen to Claire's part," said Nicky. He read out loud, in a babyish voice, "'The cat ate the mouse.'"

Mal and Jessi exchanged glances and tried very, very hard not to giggle.

"I mean, what does that have to do with anything?" asked Nicky indignantly. "There's no cat in the story."

"It's the only word I know how to write!" Claire howled. "I can't help it. Anyway, I think your story is stupid." She curled up on Mal's lap and stuck her tongue out at Nicky.

"Okay, okay," said Mal. "Time out. There has to be a solution to this problem."

"I think I have one," said Jessi. "Claire, would you like to try making a picture poem?"

"What's a picture poem?" asked Claire suspiciously.

"It's an illustration of a poem you've made up in your head," said Jessi. "You don't have to write at all."

"I can just draw?" asked Claire.

"That's right," said Jessi. "And if you want someone to write down your poem for you, maybe Nicky or Margo could help." She raised her eyebrows at them, and they nodded.

Claire climbed off of Mal's lap and started to rummage around in the crayon drawer.

"I think I've solved another problem," said Mal, who had picked up the book after Jessi put it down. "Here's a whole section on different kinds of poetry. It covers blank verse, sonnets, quatrains — whatever those are — and every other kind of poem there is. I'll show it to Vanessa, so she'll see that not all poems have to rhyme. And once she's studied this book and learned about poetry, she'll make a perfect emcee for our poetry slam."

"Excellent idea!" said Jessi.

By the end of that afternoon, all the kids were content, and the Pike house was (relatively) quiet, as everyone wrote and wrote and wrote.

Or, as Vanessa put it later, "Poems are great, and poems are fun, poems make life better for everyone!"

CHAPTER 9

Everyone agreed that we have an official mystery on our hands, which means it's time for the mystery Notebook, so here I go. Unfortunately, there are so few clues in this case that my entry won't take long....

The mystery notebook is another BSC tradition. Remember when I said that the BSC has helped to solve a bunch of mysteries? Well, after the first few, we figured we needed a central place to keep track of clues and suspects and things. (Up until then, everybody had made notes on whatever was handy: paper napkins, math tests, etc. It wasn't a very efficient system.) Now, whenever we have something important to write about a mystery we're working on, we do it in the mystery notebook. And, once I started writing about the mystery of Eli's appearance, everybody else did, too. The notebook was passed around a lot for a few days.

My first entry was about some sleuthing I did to follow up on the one measly little clue I'd turned up so far: that drugstore receipt I'd found in the driveway.

I had almost forgotten all about it. Then, after school on Tuesday (the same day that Jessi and Mal were having so much fun at the Pikes'), I suddenly remembered.

I ran home from school, as usual, and went inside to find Erin playing peek-a-boo with Eli on the couch. He was gurgling with laughter as she hid her face behind a pillow and said, "Where's Erin? Where's Erin?" When she pulled the pillow aside and said, "There she is!" Eli's face would light up with this huge smile. Obviously, he was very satisfied with his nanny.

I couldn't find anything to dislike about Erin, either, although you wouldn't find me smiling at her quite so happily. I still thought her behavior was odd. For instance, one day I walked into the kitchen while she was reaching into the lowest vegetable drawer. "Hi, Erin," I'd said. That was all. But you'd have thought I'd pulled a machine gun on her. She straightened up fast, blushed, stammered, and finally just ran out of the kitchen.

Anyway, she and Eli were happy together, and that was the most important thing. I knew there was no way we could have kept Eli without her help, so I tried to overlook her behavior.

That day, I said hi to Erin and I bent down to greet Eli. "Hello, snugglebear," I said softly, rubbing noses with him. "How's my little pumpkin?"

He smiled up at me, a little cross-eyed since our faces were so close, and I could have sworn it was a special "Hi, Abby" smile. My heart melted. I was falling more and more in love with that boy every day.

It wasn't easy to turn away from him, but I'd run hard that afternoon and I was more than ready for a hot shower before settling down with my homework. I gave Eli one last kiss on the cheek and headed upstairs.

After my shower, I decided I'd better do some laundry. With a baby in the house, the dirty clothes sure were adding up fast. I began to gather my clothes and throw them into a pile. That's when I found the receipt. It was in the pocket of a pair of jeans I hadn't worn for a week, just where I'd stuck it the night I'd found it.

When I discovered it, I forgot about the laundry and sat down to think. A drugstore receipt wasn't much of a clue, I knew that, but what other leads did we have? None. We had a baby in our house, and nobody knew where he'd come from, and unless I started to work harder on figuring things out we might *never* know. Oh, sure, the police were on the case, but how could they track down Eli's mother? It wasn't as if they had many clues, either.

Anyway, it didn't take me long to figure out what I had to do. My first order of business was to make sure that the receipt really *was* a clue, and that it wasn't just something my mother had dropped. I looked at the receipt more closely and noticed that it was for a prescription that had been filled at the drugstore's pharmacy. Then without allowing myself to pause, I reached for the phone and dialed the number under the store's name at the top of the receipt. I hadn't thought about what I was going to say but when the man at the other end said hello, the words just tumbled out of me.

"Hello," I said, trying to sound older than thirteen. "This is Rachel Stevenson. I'd like to order a refill for my prescription, please."

"Hold on just a moment, and I'll connect you with our pharmacy," said the man. A few seconds later (my heart was thudding while I waited), another man picked up the phone and I repeated what I'd said. I didn't know what I'd do if he asked me what the prescription was *for*, since I didn't have the faintest idea.

"Hold on, Ms. Stevenson," he said. I heard the faint clicking of computer keys as he tried to look up the prescription. There was a pause and then more clicking. Then he came back on to the line. "I'm sorry," he said, "but I can't seem to find your name in our files. Are you sure you have the right pharmacy?"

"Oh, yes," I said. "I'm sure. Maybe you have me under my maiden name — Goldberg?" I knew my mother sometimes used that name. If I wanted to make sure the receipt wasn't hers I had to check everything.

"Hold on," he said. More clicking. "No, I'm sorry," he said. "I have an M. Goldberg, but no Rachel here anywhere."

"Okay, well, thanks," I said. I hung up, disappointed. Sure, I'd proved that the receipt didn't belong to my mother, but *now* what? How was I going to find out where it had come from? My one little clue was really nothing but a big dead end.

Monday: No baby sighted
Tues: No baby.
Weds: N.B.
Thurs: This is becoming predictable.

Jessi and Mal spent the week doing their best to find out more about the woman from their writing class. They hovered around her before and after class, listening to conversations. They found out where she worked and trailed her whenever they could in the afternoons, after school. And every day they became more and more suspicious.

Why?

Because no matter where they saw her, no matter what time of day it was, they noticed one thing. She never had a baby with her.

She never picked up a baby from the sitter's, or brought a baby to writing group. She never bought baby food or diapers at the grocery store, and she walked right by the kids' clothing store without even looking in the windows.

She was definitely, they thought, acting like a woman who had given up her baby.

Then there was that conversation they overheard at the dry cleaner's. They'd followed their suspect in without her seeing them. As Jessi and Mal hovered behind a display on fur storage, the woman at the counter asked her how her little boy was.

"Little boy?" asked the woman. "I — I don't have a little boy. You must have me mixed up with someone else."

Jessi and Mal noted how flustered she was. It seemed to them that she was acting guilty, like someone who had something to hide. But had she really, really left her baby on our doorstep? Until they had solid proof, there was no way they could be sure.

Friday

Mal, you and Jessi can talk all you want about your suspect, but I think you're on the wrong trail. Personally, I'm convinced that the guilty party is sticking close to the scene of the crime....

Kristy had her own ideas about the mystery. From the very first time she met Eli's nanny, she was sure that she was somehow involved.

It wasn't that she thought Erin was Eli's mother, but she was certain that Erin was somehow mixed up in his appearance. "She knows something," Kristy insisted, her eyes narrowing. "And even though she doesn't have her own car, I'll bet anything she knows someone with a green one."

Kristy came to my house on Friday afternoon with Emily Michelle. I brought them into the living room. "You loves babies, don't you, Emily?" Kristy said, as she helped her little sister pull off her sweater.

"Baby!" said Emily Michelle, who isn't much of a talker yet. She reached for Eli.

Erin, who was holding him on her lap, smiled. "Isn't she adorable," she said. Eli waved his hands at Emily Michelle and grinned his terrific baby grin.

I offered to make us all a snack and headed for the kitchen. I knew Kristy wanted to "observe" Erin. I had poured out some apple juice and was just cutting up a bar of cheese when Kristy burst into the kitchen.

"That's it!" she said. "That woman is definitely involved."

It took me awhile to calm her down. "What did she say?" I asked. "Did she confess to something?"

"Practically," said Kristy. "She called him E. J."

"E. J.?" I repeated. "What do you mean?"

"She called the baby E. J. — as if she knew him by another name." Kristy's eyes were bright. "It was like a slip of the tongue, but I caught her! And I didn't let her off easily, either."

"What did you do?" I asked.

"I asked her why she'd called him that."

"And?"

"She gave me some lame excuse about having a nephew by that name who looks just like Eli," Kristy said, raising her eyebrows. "I mean, come on!"

"She does have a nephew," I said, remembering something she'd said the first night she came by.

"She *says* she has a nephew," Kristy replied. She was convinced that Erin knew something, and she was determined to find out what it was.

Well, gang, we haven't found out much, have we? But good work, everybody— and let's keep on working. We'll solve this mystery soon, I'm sure of it!

Actually, I wasn't so sure. I was more than a little discouraged.

Especially after I paid a visit to Sergeant Johnson, hoping to pry some information out of him, and left the police station feeling as clueless (literally) as ever. He was friendly, but obviously had nothing to tell me about his investigation.

I knew my fellow BSC members needed a pep talk, though, so I did my best to supply it. If we kept plugging away, we would solve the mystery soon enough.

CHAPTER 10

"Sherry?"

"No, Sherry's on vacation. This is Lucinda. Can I help you?"

"I'm looking for Ms. Stevenson." It felt funny to use that name. Usually when I call my mother at work, Sherry answers and I just ask if my mom's there. Sherry knows me and always asks about my most recent soccer game, or about whether I've met any nice boys lately. Then she connects me with Mom.

"I'm sorry," said Lucinda (though I have to say she didn't sound sorry at all). "Ms. Stevenson is away from the office right now, on family business."

Family business? What on earth was that supposed to mean? "Do you know exactly where she went?" I asked.

"I'm sorry, but I don't," answered Lucinda in her insincere way.

"Do you know when she'll be back?"

"She didn't leave that information with me." Lucinda was beginning to sound annoyed.

"Okay, well — thanks," I said. I hung up, feeling frustrated and a little suspicious. What was my mom up to? More and more often, lately, I'd been having this feeling that she was hiding something from me. I made up my mind to confront her when she arrived home.

I didn't mind that I hadn't been able to speak to her. I'd just wanted to ask if it was all right for me to pick up a few videos. It was Friday (soon after Kristy and Emily Michelle had left, and Erin had gone for the weekend), and I was preparing for the BSC sleepover I was throwing that night. I'd made a pan of brownies and checked on our supplies of ice cream, soda, and popcorn. I'd cleaned up the living room, which was where we were going to sleep, and set out some of my favorite CDs.

The only thing left to do was pick up the videos (I'd just have to go ahead and do it, without Mom's permission) and order the pizza. I could grab the videos on the way back from our BSC meeting, if Charlie wouldn't mind stopping for five minutes, and I could order the pizza as soon as I arrived home. Everything was set.

Two hours later, the meeting was over. We'd discussed the case, of course, and also nailed down final plans for the poetry slam. I was home again with videos in hand. I'd just called in an order for two large pizzas and was about to start putting out paper plates and napkins when my mom walked in, home from work (or wherever) and looking especially tired.

"Hi, sweetie," she said, dumping her briefcase on the kitchen table and picking up the mail. "How was your day?" She leafed through the mail and then threw it back onto the table with a sigh.

I almost kept quiet. After all, she looked as if she'd had a hard day. But I had to know where she'd been when I called. "Where were you this afternoon?" I asked, folding my arms.

"What?" she asked. "I was at work, of course."

"Not at four-thirty, you weren't," I said. "I called, and that Lucinda person said you were out on 'family business.'"

My mother looked surprised. Then she rolled her eyes. "Oh, Lucinda. She's a temp. She's always making mistakes."

Why wouldn't my mother look me in the eyes? Why had she picked up the mail again, even though she'd already looked through it? Why was she acting so edgy? I felt more suspicious than ever — and a little angry. "Mom, what's going on? Why won't you tell me?"

I saw something change in my mother's

face. "Oh, Abby," she said. She looked very uncomfortable. "It's complicated. It's — "

The doorbell rang. I waited for a second, hoping Anna would answer it. But she was upstairs practicing and probably hadn't heard it. I looked at my mother. "What?" I asked. "Tell me!"

"Later," said my mother. "It sounds as if your friends must be here. Go on and answer the door." She seemed relieved, but I felt frustrated.

When I opened the door, Mary Anne and Claudia were standing on the porch. "Hey!" I said. "Come on in." I opened the door wide, resolving to put the episode with my mom behind me and just enjoy the sleepover.

"Where's Eli?" asked Mary Anne. "I brought him something." She held up a colorful pillow that looked like a miniature quilt.

"He's sleeping," I said. "That is so cute. Did you make it?" I knew she had. Mary Anne loves to sew.

She started telling me where she'd found the pattern and the fabric, but just then the doorbell rang again, and Jessi and Mal came in. Soon after, Stacey showed up, and right behind her was Kristy. The BSC sleepover was in full swing.

Anna joined us as we gathered in the living room. My mom disappeared after saying a quick hello to my friends. I knew she'd check on Eli and then head into her study for a little more work. (Yup, even on a Friday night. She never knows when to stop.)

The pizza came, so we all moved into the kitchen. Since everybody in the club likes different toppings, I'd ordered it plain. But I'd also spent some time cutting up veggies, putting out oregano and parmesan, and slicing pepperoni. I laid everything out on the table, and we settled down to the very important business of pigging out.

Anna asked about BSC business, and we filled her in on BSC Writing Month. Before long, Mal was making us laugh with her rendition of the triplets' latest epic poem: "The Prince of Puke Meets Lady Lost-Her-Lunch."

For a little while, I forgot about my mother's behavior and about the mystery of Eli.

Then the phone rang. I answered it, only to find that my mother had picked up at the same time. I stayed on the line for a second, hoping to find out who it was, but my mother told me to hang up. "Right now, Abby," she said.

As if I had tried to listen in on her conversation or something. Man! I met Anna's eyes as I hung up, and she smiled sympathetically. Maybe she knew something about what was up with my mom. I had to talk to her.

I hurried my friends back into the living room and popped a movie into the VCR. It was a new one, about a talking dog. As soon as everybody was settled in to watch, I nudged Anna. "Let's go check on Eli," I whispered.

She must have known I wanted to talk to her, because she didn't hesitate. She followed me upstairs and into Mom's room. Mom was down the hall in her study, with the door closed. I could hear her voice, so I knew she was still on the phone.

"What is going on with her?" I asked Anna.

"With Mom? I don't know. She is so preoccupied, though," said Anna, looking puzzled. "I think it has to do with Eli."

We both looked over at him. He was fast asleep in his crib, and he looked incredibly peaceful and sweet.

"Isn't he the best?" I said. "I wish he was our baby brother."

"Oh, I know," cried Anna. "I love him. But we can't keep him forever."

"I can't believe we've even been allowed to keep him this long," I said. "I wonder how Mom arranged that."

"We may never know," Anna said, laughing.

We're familiar with our mother's habit of keeping things to herself. "She loves Eli too," I observed.

"She sure does," said Anna. "Have you ever caught her when she thinks she's alone with him? She makes goo-goo eyes and kissy noises, and she talks baby talk — "

"I know!" I said. "It's amazing." We were quiet for a moment, and I just knew — it was one of those twin things — that Anna was thinking the same thing I was. We felt a tiny bit jealous of Eli. Our mother is not normally a demonstrative person. Oh, we know she loves us. But hugging and all that? It's not her thing.

"Oh, well." Anna sighed. "It's still been wonderful to have Eli here."

"Speaking of whom," I said, nodding toward the crib. Eli was stretching and yawning. "Let's bring him downstairs and show him off." I smiled at Anna, glad we'd had a chance to talk, even if she didn't know any more about what was up with our mom than I did.

When we brought Eli downstairs, Kristy jumped up and hit the "pause" button on the VCR. "Forget about the movie," she said. "Here's the main attraction right now." She held out her arms for him, and everybody gathered around to coo over Eli.

Have you ever seen that movie *Three Men and a Baby*? Well, this was *Seven Sitters and a Baby*, and all eight of us were very, very happy. We fed him. We fought over who should change his diaper. (We all *wanted* to, believe it or not!) Mary Anne swore he smiled a special smile at her because she'd made him the pillow. Stacey played peek-a-boo with him. Jessi did *pliés* for him, and Mal told him a story she'd made up on the spot. Claudia let him play with one of her dangly earrings, and Kristy started explaining the rules of baseball to him.

It was as if Eli were the official mascot of the BSC.

He just sat there, loving it all. He gurgled and smiled and burped on cue. Then, suddenly, he decided it was time to go back to sleep. That's how babies are. I carried him upstairs and, after one last kiss, I laid him in his crib.

When I returned to the living room, I found my friends gathered around Anna, who was showing them the photo album from our Bat Mitzvah. I squeezed in next to her on the couch as we paged through.

"Check out Kristy in a dress!" said Stacey. She nudged Kristy. "You looked terrific that day."

Kristy blushed.

"Who's that cute guy?" asked Claudia. "I don't remember seeing him."

"That's Danny. His mom is our mom's best friend from college. He's totally obnoxious," I answered. "Going out with him would be like going out with one of the Pike triplets. No offense, Mal."

"None taken," said Mal. "I wouldn't want to go out with my brothers, either."

"Did all your relatives come to the party?" asked Mary Anne.

"Most of them," said Anna.

"All the ones we're speaking to, anyway," I said. Everybody laughed. Then Kristy started in on a story about her aunt Colleen, who has a bit of a wild streak and sometimes drives Kristy's mom nuts. Claudia topped that story with one about something her aunt Peaches had done as a kid, and soon we were all laughing uncontrollably.

There's nothing like a sleepover with good friends to take your mind off anything that's bothering you. I mean, how can you worry when you're gorging on brownies and ice cream, laughing at dumb jokes, giggling at some silly movie, and shrieking over the wacky hairstyles in the latest issue of your favorite magazine? Trust me, you can't. I just laughed the night away.

Saturday

Malory, if your reading this, I have one quesion. Are you sure you whant to be a writter when you grow up? I never new what a hard job it is.

But Claud, the kids all ended up having fun, didn't they?

Sure. But I think I'll stick to art and leav writting to the rest of you.

Considering the way you spell, maybe that's not a bad idea. (Only Kidding! Pals???)

Claudia wasn't offended by Stacey's kidding. She knows she can't spell, and she doesn't much care. To her, it's a mystery that anybody would want to be a writer, especially after she saw the torture (all right, maybe that's a little melodramatic, but you'll see what I mean) some of the kids were going through.

Claudia showed up at the Arnold house on Saturday afternoon just in time to find Marilyn and Carolyn, the identical twins (they're eight years old), in the middle of a huge quarrel. Claudia could hear their angry voices the second she walked in the door.

"I'm sorry, but we have to run," said Mrs. Arnold apologetically, before Claudia had even taken off her jacket.

Mr. Arnold looked a little sheepish, too, but he pointed to his watch. "We have a train to catch," he said. The Arnolds were going to Manhattan for the afternoon and evening.

"They'll make up any minute, I'm sure," said Mrs. Arnold brightly.

"It's all right," Claudia said, shooing them out the door. "It's all part of being a babysitter. I'm used to sibling squabbles. Don't worry about a thing." The Arnolds looked relieved as they left. Claudia shut the door behind them and turned toward the sound of the twins' voices.

She found the girls in the living room. Marilyn was twirling around on the piano stool, making nasty faces at her sister. Carolyn was making identical nasty faces in return.

The Arnold girls really do look an awful lot alike. In fact, I've heard that when the BSC first started to sit for them, nobody could tell them apart, partly because they used to dress alike too. Sitters used to have to rely on the fact that Marilyn has a tiny mole under her right eye, while Carolyn has one under her left. But, over time, the twins made it clear to their mom that they wanted to express their individual personalities more, and now it's easier to tell at a glance which one is which.

Marilyn is the more outgoing twin. She wears her brown hair longer now and dresses in simple, comfortable outfits. She takes piano lessons and plays very well.

Carolyn, who has a trendier haircut and is a lot more fashion conscious, couldn't be less interested in music. Her passion is science. She wants to be a scientist when she grows up. Not long ago, she "invented" a time machine and charged kids money to take a ride in it! (The kids all got their money back in the end.)

"Those are too my socks," Carolyn was saying, as Claudia entered the room. She was glaring at Marilyn, who stuck out her feet as if to show off the lace-trimmed anklets she was wearing.

"Are not," said Marilyn. "You had a pair like them, but you lost one, remember? And Mom bought me these. They're mine!"

"You stole them!"

"Did not."

"Did too! And now you're lying about it."

"Whoa, time out!" said Claudia. "Do you two realize that you're fighting about a pair of socks? What's it going to be next, who has the best toothbrush?"

The girls giggled in spite of themselves.

"Actually, Marilyn does have a really cool toothbrush," Carolyn said thoughtfully.

"It's just like yours!" said Marilyn.

"No, yours is purple," said Carolyn. "Mine's that stupid green color. I hate it. Why do you always get the better stuff? Mom always buys you exactly what you want."

"That's not true!" cried Marilyn. "Don't you remember when we were in the supermarket yesterday and she let you choose the cookies?"

They were off and running all over again. Claudia rolled her eyes. The twins would probably argue all day unless she came up with something better to do. That's when she remembered BSC Writing Month.

"Hey, you guys," she said, after she'd whistled loudly enough to grab their attention and stop their bickering. "I have a great idea. You know about Writing Month, right?"

The twins nodded.

"Well, how about if we have a writing workshop today?" asked Claudia. "We can even have some other kids over. I know Stacey is sitting at the Johanssens', and Charlotte would probably love to come."

"I'll call her!" said Marilyn.

"I'll put out all our supplies and stuff!" said Carolyn.

Claudia smiled to herself. Her idea had worked. Little did she know that her troubles had just begun.

It turned out that Becca Ramsey was visiting Charlotte, and both of them agreed that a writing workshop sounded like fun. Stacey brought the girls over, and everybody gathered around the table in the kitchen.

Claudia and Stacey told me later that they thought poetry writing would make a perfect activity. After all, those four girls like to write. But it turned out, as Claudia and Stacey discovered, that there can be a big difference between liking to write and being a Writer. And because of the upcoming prose party/poetry slam, the girls were feeling a certain amount of pressure. This wasn't just writing for fun anymore.

This was the big time.

Everything was set up for a great afternoon of writing. Carolyn had rounded up a bunch of pads and had set out handfuls of pens and newly sharpened pencils. She'd also found a dictionary, a thesaurus, and a book of baby names. "In case people need names for their characters," she explained.

"Good thinking," Claudia said, impressed.

"So, we're all set," declared Stacey. "Let the writing begin!" She was trying to sound cheerful, because she could already see that the girls weren't altogether happy. Something wasn't right. Not one of them even reached to pick up a pen.

"What's the matter?" asked Claudia.

At that, all four girls started to talk at once.

"I have writer's block," wailed Marilyn.

"I don't know how to decide what to read," said Charlotte, holding up a huge pile of papers she'd brought along.

"How can I read these poems out loud?" Becca asked. "I'll die. I'll just die."

"Nobody's going to understand mine," Carolyn said, shaking her head sadly.

Claudia and Stacey exchanged glances.

"Okay, let's try to help each other out," said Stacey. "That's what a workshop is for, right?" She looked around at four miserable faces. "Come on, guys, this is supposed to be fun," she added.

"Writing *is* fun," said Charlotte. "But trying to figure out what other people will like is so hard." She pointed to the pile of papers. "I like my poems best, but my parents looked bored when I was reading them out loud last night. Now I think it might be better to read a story, but which one?"

"I wish I had your problem," said Marilyn, looking enviously at the pile. "If I had that much stuff to choose from, I'd be happy. I can't even think of one thing to write about."

"I can," said Becca in a small voice. "But everything I write is kind of personal. I can't even imagine reading it out loud onstage." She looked terrified.

"I don't mind being onstage," said Carolyn, "but the stuff I write is all scientific. I want to try to explain about photosynthesis — you know, why plants are green. We just learned about that in school. But I have a feeling that the little kids won't be able to understand what I'm talking about."

Everybody fell silent. They knew Carolyn was probably right.

Then, suddenly, Claudia grinned. "I have an idea," she said slowly. "I have a really great idea. An idea that might solve all your problems."

Stacey was relieved. "What? Tell us."

"A play," said Claudia. "You four should

write a play together. It'll be perfect!"

Silence. But Claudia didn't let the gloom stop her. "Look, it'll work. Charlotte, you can't decide what piece to read for everyone. Well, how about a play? It's made to be performed in front of an audience, so they won't be bored. And Marilyn, I bet you could lose that writer's block if you were bouncing ideas off the others and working with them. Becca, this'll help you with your stage fright, because you won't be up there alone. And Carolyn, you — you — " Claudia paused. She had it figured out — except for Carolyn's part.

"Maybe the play could help explain photosynthesis," Stacey said. "If it was presented in a fun way, maybe the little kids would understand."

Claudia shot Stacey a grateful glance. And then the two of them looked expectantly at the girls, and saw four smiling faces.

"Yes!" cried Marilyn. "We can do it!"

"Let's start right now!" said Becca.

"This'll be great," added Carolyn.

"Act One, Scene One," said Charlotte, reading the words aloud as she wrote them.

Claudia and Stacey gave each other high fives. Their writing workshop was a success. And, if all went well, the girls' play would be a big hit. Even if it *was* about photosynthesis.

CHAPTER 12

"**W**as that a sneeze?" I ran to Eli's crib. "Oh, poor baby," I said, reaching down to rub his belly. Eli looked miserable. It was Sunday, and in the twenty-four hours since my BSC sleepover, Eli had come down with a cold. He'd been sneezing and sniffling and coughing — and crying. A lot. We had one unhappy baby on our hands.

My mom had called our pediatrician, Dr. Hernandez, to ask for advice. There wasn't much we could do besides making sure he drank lots of fluids, and keeping an eye on him. If he developed a fever, we were supposed to call Dr. Hernandez again.

I felt Eli's forehead. "He's a little warm," I said. "Mom, feel him. Don't you think he's warmer?"

"I just felt him five minutes ago," said my mother impatiently. "He's fine, Abby. It's just a cold." She was sitting on her bed, paging through her address book.

I'd barely seen or talked to Mom in what seemed like days. It was almost as if she were avoiding me. On Friday she'd started to tell me something, and when we were interrupted she promised to talk to me soon. But so far, I hadn't heard a word. She'd been acting very preoccupied, and it seemed as if she spent most of her time holed up in her study, making secretive phone calls.

I knew it all must have something to do with Eli, but as far as details went, I was still clueless, and I had the feeling my mom liked it that way. A couple of times I tried to remind her that she'd promised to talk to me, but she brushed me off. And I knew better than to push her too hard. My mother is not a person who reacts well to being pushed.

Eli sniffled. "Mom," I began. "Don't you think — "

"Abby, he's *fine*. Just relax." Mom stood up. "I'll be in my study, but please don't interrupt me unless there's a *real* emergency." She smiled, but only with her mouth. Her eyes looked serious.

I understood what she was saying. She didn't want to hear about it every time Eli sneezed. "Okay," I said, shrugging.

She left the room, and I went back to hovering over Eli. He was sleeping, but not very soundly. He tossed his head back and forth, clenched his little fists, and frowned as he tried to breathe through his tiny stuffed-up nose. Poor guy. It's bad enough to have a cold when you're grown-up and understand what's happening to you. But Eli didn't know what had hit him, or why I couldn't make him feel better.

It broke my heart.

He sneezed again, but it was just a little sneeze and he didn't even wake up. Still, the sneeze made me wonder if he was feeling worse. I put my hand on his forehead again and tried to decide if it was warmer.

Suddenly I heard my mother's study door open and shut. Then I heard quick footsteps coming down the hall. She poked her head into the room. "I have to go out," she said. "You and Anna have to take care of Eli."

"Huh?" I asked. "Where are you going? What — "

"No time to talk," my mom called over her shoulder, as she headed for the stairs. "I'll phone you later."

Okay. Did I say my mom was acting strange before? Well, that was nothing. Now her behavior had become totally bizarre. Never before had she taken off on a Sunday afternoon without saying where she was going or why.

I followed her down the stairs, trying to form a question. But before I could put the words together, she was gone. I stood there gaping at the closed front door.

"What is going *on* with her?" Anna asked from behind me. She was wiping her hands on a kitchen towel. "I was in there making lunch, and the next thing I know she flies down the stairs and out the door. She barely took the time to tell me she was going out — but she didn't say where, or — or — " Anna looked stunned.

"Or why, or anything," I finished. "I know. She's up to something, and I'm tired of being kept in the dark." It was time to take action. "I'm going to go snoop in her study."

"Abby, no!" said Anna. "That's not right."

"I don't care. It's not right for her to keep secrets from us, either. Especially if they're about Eli. We have a right to know." I'd made up my mind. You know, you don't become captain of your soccer team unless you're willing to make decisions and stand by them. I've never been a wishy-washy person, and I probably never will be.

I turned and headed upstairs, not caring whether Anna was following me or not. I marched into my mother's study and over to her desk.

Where to start?

I ran my gaze over the messy desktop. My mother is not the most organized person in the world. There were piles of mail waiting to be opened, stacks of manuscripts waiting to be read, and, sprinkled over everything like seasoning, dozens of black fine-point felt-tip pens, the only kind my mom ever uses.

There was also a vase of yellow tulips that had seen their best days about a week ago, several postcards from a friend who was apparently vacationing on some tropical island, and a picture of me and Anna in our Bat Mitzvah dresses. The tulips made me sneezy, but I ignored my runny nose. I had detective work to do.

An appointment book lay open in the middle of the chaos, and I zeroed in for a better look. The space for Sunday was totally blank.

Major frustration. My mother's study wasn't giving up its secrets any more easily than she was giving up hers.

I sat down on her desk chair and twirled around, thinking. Then, on my third twirl (I was beginning to feel a little nauseous), something caught my eye. A square of bright yellow, next to the phone. It was a Post-It note. I stopped twirling and took a closer look. There was only one word on the yellow square. One word, written in my mother's handwriting, with one of those black fine-point felt-tip pens.

Miriam.

Miriam! Why did that name ring a bell? I said it out loud. "Miriam." Who was Miriam?

Suddenly, I remembered. Miriam was my mother's younger sister.

You may think it's strange that I could have forgotten that my mother has a sister. It's not, though. Here's why: Nobody in our family has spoken to Miriam in years. Not only that, nobody talks *about* her. Not even her parents, my grandparents.

I'm not sure what Miriam did — or didn't do — to make everyone so mad at her. Thinking back, I had vague memories of my mother complaining that Miriam was so irresponsible, and that she always expected Mom to bail her out when she found herself in trouble.

Miriam.

I jumped up and ran downstairs to find Anna. She had gone back into the kitchen. I burst through the door, holding up the sticky note. "Miriam!" I said. "Mom's sister."

"What about her?" asked Anna.

"I don't know," I confessed. "All I know is that Mom wrote her name down. That must mean something."

"We don't know anything about her," said Anna. "I don't even know what she looks like."

We glanced at each other, then flew off toward the living room. (Twin communication. Cool, huh?)

Within seconds, we'd pulled all the photo albums off the shelf and were paging through them wildly. "She wasn't at our Bat Mitzvah, we know that," I said, throwing that album aside. I didn't even remember Miriam's name being mentioned when we were discussing the guest list.

"I don't see her in this one," said Anna. "And it goes back at least four years." She sounded sad. I looked up and saw that she was going through a brown leather album. I knew it was one that included pictures of the last family vacation we'd taken before our dad died. We'd gone to this island in Maine where we'd stayed in a cottage on the beach. . . .

I threw Anna another album. We didn't have time to waste on nostalgia. "Check this one out," I said.

We raced through the pictures. It was like looking at a speeded-up movie of our lives. Like those time-lapse films of flowers blooming and trees growing. Only these were pictures of two girls who grew. It took me about ten minutes to chart our course from babyhood (identical bundles in identical bassinets) to toddler times to those gawky ten-year-old moments.

The books were also full of pictures of our grandparents, and of my father's relatives. But nowhere, nowhere, were there pictures of anyone who might be Miriam.

"Look at this picture of Mom and Grandpa Morris and Gram Elsie," said Anna. "It almost looks as if someone cut part of the picture out, doesn't it?" She showed me a picture in one of the older albums, from before we were born. Mom looked about twenty years old.

She was right. And if I had to guess, I'd bet that the missing part had, at one time, showed Miriam. Miriam, the other daughter.

"Let's go back even further," I said. "Let's look at the ones from Mom's childhood." I pulled two old red leather albums off the shelf and handed one to Anna. We started to page through, looking at the black-and-white crinkle-edged photos. And then, almost immediately, I hit pay dirt.

I drew in a breath. "Whoa," I said. "Check it out!" I showed Anna what I'd found. It was a picture of two children — girls — sitting on a set of concrete steps outside an apartment building. The older girl was Mom; I could tell by the shape of her nose and the slant of her eyebrows. She must have been seven or eight. The younger girl was about four. She was squinting at the camera and sucking her thumb. She was also clutching a blanket.

A blanket with cowboys and horses on it. Even though it looked different in black-and-white, I recognized it immediately.

"That blanket!" I said. "That's the one Eli came wrapped in. I'm sure of it."

"That must be Miriam," said Anna.

"And Miriam — Miriam must be Eli's mother!" I gasped. "Miriam Goldberg — M. Goldberg! That was *her* prescription."

"And Mom must have gone to see her," said Anna. "But where is she?"

I didn't answer.

"Abby?" asked Anna. "What's the matter?"

"I'm thinking," I said. "I was trying to figure out how we could tell where Mom went. And I think I just had a really good idea." I bolted up the stairs, headed for the phone on my mom's desk, and punched the redial button.

CHAPTER 13

The phone rang three times. Then a voice on the other end said, "St. Barnabas Hospital."

I gulped.

"What is it?" asked Anna, who was leaning over the desk, watching me closely.

I held up a finger to tell her to wait a second. "Miriam Goldberg, please," I said. My voice sounded surprisingly normal. I was glad the receptionist had no way of knowing how badly my hands were shaking.

"Is she a patient?" asked the receptionist.

How should I know? "Yes," I said, taking a wild guess. For all I knew, she might be a brain surgeon.

"Hold, please," said the receptionist. I heard a click, then some syrupy music. Still holding the phone to my ear, I looked up at Anna. "She's in the hospital," I said.

"For what?" asked Anna.

I shrugged. "Maybe — " I began, but just

then the receptionist came back on the line.

"I'm sorry, the nurse says Ms. Goldberg is sleeping right now," she said.

"I see," I answered. "Thank you."

"Good-bye," said the receptionist.

"Wait!" I said. "Can you tell me how to find St. Barnabas from Grand Central Station?"

"Certainly." She ran down the directions, and I scribbled them on a scrap of paper. I thanked her, hung up, and turned to Anna.

"I'm going to New York," I said.

"Oh, right," said Anna. "Sure."

"No, really. I am. I want some answers, and I want them now. I'm not going to wait for Mom to come home and act all mysterious again. This time I'm going to find out for myself what's going on. I owe it to Eli."

"But you can't — " Anna began.

"Sure I can," I interrupted. "We've taken the train to the city before. It's no big deal."

"You've never done it alone," Anna pointed out.

"So?" I asked. "There's always a first time." I was trying hard to sound matter-of-fact, even though I was scared to death. It was true that I'd never been to the city by myself before.

"Mom will kill you," said Anna. "You'll be grounded for fifteen years."

"We'll see. All I know is that I have to go."

Anna realized I was serious. "Well, if you're

really going, then I'm going, too," she said. "I don't want you to go alone."

"I'm going to have to, though. Somebody has to stay with Eli," I pointed out. Erin was off on Sundays.

Anna knew there was no use arguing. I was determined, and when I feel that way, nobody can stop me.

I picked up the phone again and called the train station to check on the Sunday schedule. There was a train leaving in forty-five minutes, which gave me plenty of time. Next, I called Bud's Taxi and said I needed a cab in half an hour. After that, I headed up to my room to change.

Finally, I went into my mom's room, where Eli lay sleeping. "He seems to be breathing a little easier," said Anna.

"Don't forget to check his temperature every hour," I reminded her, even though I knew she'd be just as responsible about taking care of him as I would have been. I stroked his soft cheek. "I'm going to see your mommy," I told him. "At least, I think I am. And I'm going to find out why she left you with us." After that, what? I had no idea. I just knew I had to make sure Eli would always be taken care of.

I kissed him one last time and said good-bye to Anna.

"Good luck. And be careful!"

"I will. Don't worry." Just then, the cab honked outside, and I had to run.

It was a quick trip to the train station, and I arrived just as the train pulled in. I paid the driver, thanked him, and dashed for the train.

Ten minutes later, the train pulled slowly out of the station and I was on my way to New York.

By myself!

Now that I had time to think, I began to wonder whether this was really such a great idea. It's not as if I know my way around Manhattan. It would be easy to get lost. Not to mention all the other things that could happen to me, things too scary to even think about. My brain was racing, and I began to feel dizzy with nervousness.

To take my mind off my fears, I made myself think about Miriam. I tried to remember everything I knew about her, which wasn't much. I knew she was several years younger than my mother, and that once when they were little girls they had eaten so much licorice that they'd both thrown up. (That was a story my mom would tell me and Anna when we were younger and begged her constantly for candy.)

I knew Miriam had had a turtle named Mabel (my mother's turtle, Mabel's twin, was named Doris). And I knew she had won an essay contest when she was in fifth grade, because my mother told me how jealous she'd felt whenever Miriam showed off her blue ribbon.

Most of the stories I remembered about Miriam were about what she was like as a young girl. All I could recall about the teenage Miriam was that she had a way of attracting "bad" boys — boys with motorcycles, boys who kept her out late. She must have held the world's record for being grounded, according to my mom.

And the adult Miriam? I was pretty sure I'd only met her once, when Anna and I were maybe four years old. I had a vague memory of a nice lady with a blonde ponytail, a lady who laughed and joked and bought us ice-cream cones. But I couldn't bring her face into focus, and I couldn't remember where we were or why we spent an afternoon with her.

She didn't come to my father's funeral. I remembered hearing that she was out of the country at the time. And as far as I knew, she had been totally out of touch with my mom and my grandparents for at least the last few years.

It was strange to think that I had an aunt I knew next to nothing about.

It was even stranger to think that Eli might be my cousin.

But I was jumping the gun, getting ahead of myself. I didn't know anything for sure, except that I had plenty of questions and I wasn't going to let my mother avoid answering them anymore.

I was so absorbed in my thoughts that I barely noticed the train entering the tunnel under the city leading to Grand Central Station. So it was a bit of a surprise when the train ground to a halt and I looked out to see the familiar platforms.

I'd never paid much attention to how Mom found her way up the stairs and out through Grand Central. Whenever I came to the city with her, I just followed as she led the way. This time, I had to figure it out for myself. I watched to see which way most of the passengers leaving the train were going, and then I followed them up a long escalator.

Somehow I found my way out of the cavernous building and onto the street. Now all I had to do was find a cab, tell the driver the address of the hospital, and relax.

As if. There was no way I was going to relax anytime soon.

I watched the cabs fly by and tried to remember how my mother tells which ones are available for passengers. I knew it had something to do with the light on the roof of the cab, but what? And even if I did know which ones were available, how was I supposed to make one stop for me? Suddenly, I felt like crying. I'd come all this way, and now I was stuck.

"Need a cab, dearie?"

I turned to see a tiny silver-haired old woman standing next to me. She was wearing an impeccable navy blue suit and white gloves, and she was carrying a shopping bag from Bloomingdale's.

She did not look like a criminal.

I nodded. I was afraid that if I tried to talk I might start sobbing.

She put her hand on my arm. "Don't you worry," she said. She took off one of her gloves. Then she turned to look out onto the street. A whole flock of cabs was drawing closer. How was this tiny woman going to stop one of them?

Suddenly, she stuck her thumb and first finger in her mouth and gave a piercing whistle. One of the cabs pulled right over, like a dog coming to its owner. She opened the door and ushered me in. "Not very ladylike, I know," she said with a smile. "But my dear husband, Leo, taught me how to do that, and it works every time. Have a nice day!" She slammed the door shut before I could thank her.

Only in New York.

I gave the driver the address of the hospital. He took off fast and drove faster, and we were there before I knew it. I paid him, remembering to add a tip, and headed into the big marble lobby of St. Barnabas.

Inside, I felt overwhelmed all over again. This was a huge hospital. How was I going to find Miriam? "Use your brain, Abby," I muttered. I looked around and saw the main reception desk. All I had to do was ask for Miriam, and they'd tell me where to find her.

Sure enough, they did (after I waited what seemed like hours for the receptionist to page through a huge computer printout). Miriam was in room 401, and I could take the elevator located "down that hall and on the right."

I followed directions and found the elevator, but after I'd pushed the button and waited for fifteen seconds, I discovered that I was just too antsy to wait any longer. There was a stairway across from the elevator, and I pushed the door open and started climbing.

When I reached the fourth floor, I looked carefully at the signs and turned right. Room 401 turned out to be the first door I came to. It was closed.

I put my ear next to the door, hoping to hear something, but I couldn't hear a sound. Slowly, slowly, I pushed the door open.

There were two beds in the room. One was empty. But a woman was lying in the one near the window. And sitting in a chair next to that bed was my mother.

She was crying.

CHAPTER 14

"Mom?" My voice came out like a little squeak.

She looked up and wiped her eyes. "Abby," she said. She looked surprised, of course. But also *not* surprised. It was weird. She didn't ask me any of the questions I would have expected, such as "How did you get here?" or "What are you doing here alone?"

Instead, she just sort of nodded at me. "Abby," she said again, repeating my name as if she needed to remind herself of something. She turned to look at the woman in the bed. "Miriam," she said, "here's Abby to see you. Do you remember Abby?"

Miriam smiled weakly and raised a hand in greeting. "Hello, Abby," she said. "I'm your aunt Miriam."

I stepped closer to the bed. The woman lying there looked very much like my mom, only her hair was a few shades lighter. Her face was pale, and she had dark circles under her eyes. She was hooked up to an I.V. line, and she looked very sick and very tired. "Hello, Aunt Miriam," I said. Suddenly I felt a wave of emotion. This woman was related to me; she was part of my family. A part I'd never really known. I glanced at my mom and saw that she was crying again.

"Your aunt is going to be fine," she told me, in a shaky voice. "She's been extremely ill, but now that she's being taken care of properly, she'll be all right."

"And I hear my son's all right too," said Aunt Miriam. "Thanks to some very good care from — from my family." Tears were welling up in her eyes, too.

"Eli is your son?" I asked.

She smiled. "His name is Daniel. And yes, he's my boy."

"He's wonderful," I told her. Somehow I just knew that she thought so too — and that she hadn't really abandoned him.

"I know. I miss him terribly." She closed her eyes for a moment.

"Miriam, would you like to nap?" asked my mother. "We can leave you alone for a bit."

She waved a hand. "I'm all right," she said. "I'll just be quiet for a few minutes." She looked at me. "I think Abby deserves an ex-

planation, though. Maybe you can fill her in."
She closed her eyes again.

My mom turned to me and took my hand.
"Sit down," she said, gesturing to the window-
sill.

I sat.

The room was dimly lit, and the blinds on
the window behind me were drawn. It was
very quiet, even though the hall outside had
been full of bustling nurses and patients in
wheelchairs.

It was so quiet that I could almost hear my
heart beating as I waited for my mom to start
talking.

"First of all, I want you to know that Miriam
and I have put our differences behind us. I
hope you'll accept her as part of our family. I
feel awful about all the years we've wasted."
Tears began to slip down her face again.

"Mom," I said. "Tell me what's going on.
Why is Miriam in the hospital?"

My mom blew her nose on a tissue and
pulled herself together. She took a deep breath
and squared her shoulders.

"Miriam has diabetes," she began. Just like
Stacey, I thought. "Only lately she hasn't been
taking very good care of herself." She glanced
at her sister, who now appeared to be sleeping
peacefully. "Miriam has never been very good
at taking care of herself," she said softly.

"Anyway, she had Daniel six months ago — two months after she and Daniel's father broke up."

"Did you ever meet him?" I asked.

She shook her head. "No, but my parents did. They couldn't stand him. They made it clear that they didn't want anything to do with Miriam if she was going to be with him. That's why they didn't even know she was pregnant. Nobody knew."

"Where has Miriam been living all these years?" I asked.

"Everywhere," said my mom. "It sounds as if she's lived in ten states and three different countries. But after Daniel's father left her, she decided to settle down in New York and make a new life for herself."

"Why didn't we know she was here?" I asked.

"She didn't want to call me until she was back on her feet," said my mom. "She knew I was sick and tired of helping her out every time she found herself in trouble. That's why we hadn't spoken in so long." Mom shook her head and stroked Miriam's forehead. Miriam didn't open her eyes.

"So then what happened?" I asked.

"She wasn't eating right. She didn't have much money, and what she did have, she put toward Daniel's care."

I thought of the well-stocked diaper bag and nodded.

"She started to become seriously ill, and finally she decided to break down and ask me to take care of Daniel for awhile. She didn't know anyone else in the area. So she used her last few dollars to rent a car to drive her and Daniel out to Stoneybrook. By the time she found our house, she was feeling very faint. And when she knocked on the door and got no answer, she didn't know what to do. She wasn't thinking clearly, but she knew there was no way she could care for Daniel until she regained her health. So she wrote me a short note and left Daniel on the doorstep."

"A note?" I asked. "I didn't see any note."

"It was tucked into the car seat. And it was pretty incoherent. But I figured out that the baby was probably Miriam's. Especially when I saw the blanket he was wrapped in."

I remembered how she'd reacted when she'd first seen the blanket. "That was Miriam's blanket when she was little, wasn't it?" I asked, thinking of the picture I'd seen.

"It was my bankie," Miriam murmured. I looked over and saw that her eyes were open again. "I took it everywhere with me." She smiled.

"Well, I'm glad you still had it," said my mother. "Otherwise I wouldn't have been sure that Daniel was your baby. Then came the hard part — finding you." She reached out and took her sister's hand. "I looked everywhere for Miriam," she told me. "I told the police what I suspected, and they helped, but I also wanted to look on my own. I called everyone I could think of, anyone who might have heard from her. I called social service organizations all over the country. But nobody knew where she was. Finally, I thought of calling the hospitals. And that's when I found her."

"I'd been here for quite awhile by then," said Miriam. "But I was so sick when I arrived that I couldn't tell anyone much more than my name. And then I was in a coma for awhile — "

"A coma!" I said. "That sounds awful."

Miriam shrugged. "It can happen when diabetes is out of control. It's worse for the people taking care of you, though. I didn't know a thing; it was just as if I were sleeping."

"But then you woke up," said my mother gently.

"Then I woke up," agreed Miriam. "And soon after that, you found me. I promise this will be the last time you ever have to help me out like this," she said.

"I'll help you out whenever you need me," my mother said. "We're family. I don't know why I let myself forget that for so long, but now that we're back together, I'll never forget it again." She and Miriam were both crying now.

Whoa. Deep stuff, and there I was, right in the middle of it. I discovered that tears were running down my face, too.

Just then, the door swung open and a nurse looked in. "Visiting hours are over now," she said gently. "I'm going to have to ask you to let Ms. Goldberg rest."

My mom bent down to kiss her sister. "I'll see you tomorrow," she promised.

I gave Miriam a kiss, too. Even though I barely knew her, it seemed like the thing to do.

Then we left the hospital. Mom didn't say a word as we walked to the parking garage where she'd left the car. In fact, we didn't start talking until we'd made it out of the city and were on the highway headed home. I had the feeling Mom was worn out.

Finally, I broke the silence. "Mom, why didn't you tell me?" I asked. "I was going nuts trying to figure out where Eli — I mean, Daniel — came from. And you knew all the time!" I'd realized by then that Mom must have told Sergeant Johnson about the note, which was why we'd been allowed to keep Daniel. But Mom must have sworn him to secrecy.

"I wasn't absolutely sure," she said. "But

you're right. I probably should have told you. I didn't realize how much trouble and worry I was causing you. It's just that — well, nobody even knew Miriam was pregnant. I didn't think I should tell my parents anything until I'd tracked her down and found out the whole story."

"But you could have told me and Anna," I said.

"I didn't want you to have to lie to Grandpa Morris and Gram Elsie," said my mom. "It was bad enough that I had to. And I probably shouldn't have, but I just didn't want to worry them. Even though they've had very little to do with Miriam lately, she is still their daughter, and they'd be upset if they knew she was missing. It hasn't been that long since Grandpa Morris's heart surgery, you know."

I realized that this explained why my grandparents hadn't wanted to talk about the baby with me on the phone that day. Mom had probably downplayed the whole thing so much that they didn't think it was too exciting. "Will you call them now?" I asked.

"As soon as we get home," my mother said.

Thinking of home reminded me of something. "So, am I grounded or anything?" I asked. "You know, for coming to New York by myself?" I might as well find out what she had in mind.

She looked at me. Then she looked back at the road. "I can't say I approve of what you did," she said. "But I won't punish you. After all, it was partly my fault, because I didn't tell you everything I knew. What you did was wrong, but I was wrong too. I guess we're even." She looked at me again and grinned.

"Cool," I said, smiling back at her. I think we were both very glad that the secret had been revealed.

CHAPTER 15

"Pass the cream cheese, please."

"Are there any more sesame bagels?"

"This is excellent lox."

"More eggs, anyone?"

Ahh, the sounds of Sunday brunch. (For anyone who doesn't know what lox is, it's yummy smoked salmon. When you add some to a bagel and cream cheese, it's like heaven on earth.)

It was exactly a week from the day of my solo-in-Manhattan adventure, and a lot had changed. For one thing, Miriam was out of the hospital. She had come to stay with us for a bit, and seeing her and Daniel together was wonderful. It was obvious to everyone that she loved him very much, and by the way his little face lit up when he saw her, it was clear that the feeling was mutual. I almost felt jealous, but I knew that was silly. After all, Miriam was Daniel's mother. He still loved me too, but not in the same way.

I looked across the kitchen table at Daniel, who was nestled in his mother's arms. He looked totally content, even though he was too young to eat lox. I smiled at him and felt myself growing a little teary-eyed. Then I looked around the table and saw that everyone else was wearing the same sappy smile I probably had plastered across my face.

Mom wore it.

Anna did too.

Miriam? Definitely.

And the award for the biggest, sappiest smiles went to Grandpa Morris and Gram Elsie, who couldn't stop looking at their newest grandchild.

Their presence at our breakfast table represented the biggest change that had taken place that week. A family reconciliation. Mom had called her parents in Florida as soon as we'd arrived home from the hospital. She'd broken the news gently, concerned about her father's heart.

My grandparents had caught the first available flight to New York.

Somehow, Daniel's presence made it easy for everyone to forgive and forget. He was such a beautiful, lovable baby. The week had been one big love fest. The only arguments had been about whose turn it was to hold Daniel.

That was the good news. My family was one again. And now Daniel was a part of my family. I knew I should be happy about it.

But there was bad news too.

We were going to lose Daniel. Just when I'd become used to the idea of a baby in the house. He and Miriam were going to live with my grandparents for awhile, down in Florida. She insisted that she'd only stay until she was "back on her feet," but my grandparents told her she could stay as long as she'd like.

"How can you take him away?" I cried when Miriam first told me they were going.

"It's the best thing for both of us, right now," Miriam had told me gently. "I need my parents, and Daniel needs me. We'll come back and visit, though. And you should come down to Florida."

"Yes, bubbelah," put in Gram Elsie. "We'd love to have you and your sister any time."

"We'll show you the town," said Grandpa Morris with a laugh. "Bring some friends if you want. We need more young people down there!"

Right then and there, I started dreaming up a BSC trip to Florida. I knew my friends and

I could have a great time. Maybe this move wasn't such a bad idea. After all, Daniel would be in good hands. I told myself that he'd be better off with three full-time caretakers than with two thirteen-year-olds and a very busy aunt.

No matter what, I knew that Miriam and Daniel would always be a part of my life now, and that felt terrific.

Anyway, back to that Sunday brunch. By the end of it, we'd eaten so much we could barely move. But we had an important event to attend: the BSC Prose Party and Poetry Slam! The whole Goldberg-Stevenson clan was going to be on hand, including Miriam, who was just about ready for her first outing, and Daniel, who would probably sleep quietly through the event.

The party was going to take place in the main children's room of the Stoneybrook Public Library, and as soon as we walked in we saw that Claudia had done an excellent job with the decorations. The walls were covered in brightly colored cutouts of letters and punctuation marks, and crepe paper hung in huge swags from every bookshelf. There was a small "gallery" of picture poems, by Claire and other younger kids. And an area in the front of the room had been designated as the stage. Ms. Feld, the children's librarian, had helped with setting up a microphone so the audience wouldn't miss a word.

The event started on time, as Vanessa stepped onto the stage, picked up the microphone, and greeted the audience (mostly made up of parents and friends of the writers) with a rendition of a couple of her favorite poems, which she'd memorized. She talked for a minute about various forms of poetry and prose and then went on to introduce the first "act," which was the Pike triplets.

They'd written a rap about — what else? — boogers and puke. But you know what? It was pretty good, actually. Or at least memorable. I noticed several audience members, Gram Elsie included, looking a little green at first. But by the end of the performance, everyone was laughing.

The triplets were a tough act to follow, but David Michael did a terrific job reading his story about Prince Eli. After that, Melody Korman read her poem, and Maria Kilbourne told her fairy tale. I glanced at Miriam and saw that she knew the stories were about Daniel. She looked pleased and proud. Daniel, on the other hand, was sleeping soundly.

Afterward, everyone agreed that the high point of the show was the play put on by

Charlotte, Becca, Marilyn, and Carolyn. It was funny, well written, and even educational, and the acting was excellent. The best part was when Becca, dressed as a tree, sang a song about chlorophyll. I think Mary Anne even cried a little at that point. They received a standing ovation, three "curtain calls," and first prize in the contest.

Vanessa wrapped up the party by inviting everyone to stay for refreshments. Amazingly, by that time I was hungry (I thought I'd never eat again, after that brunch), and I joined my BSC friends by the food some parents had provided. Then we moved off to a corner to talk — about BSC Writing Month and how it was going to have to be an annual event; about Daniel and Miriam and how cool it was that Anna and I had discovered a new branch of our family tree; and about how happy we were that the mystery had finally been solved. There were only a few loose ends to be tied up. Erin, for one.

"What about that nanny?" asked Stacey. "If she wasn't connected with the mystery, why was she acting so weird?"

I laughed, and so did Anna.

"We figured that out," I said. "On her last day, she explained everything. It turned out that even though she'd done a lot of child care

— her references weren't made up — this was her first real job as a nanny, and she was terrified. That's why she always seemed so nervous."

"And by the way, she really did have a nephew named E. J.," Anna chimed in. "She showed me pictures, and he does look an awful lot like Daniel."

"What about that lady in your writing class?" Kristy asked, turning to Jessi and Mal.

Mal blushed, and Jessi looked down at her feet. "Well, it's kind of embarrassing," she said.

"The thing is," said Mal, "even though we should know by now that truth and fiction are two different things — "

"We forgot for a little while," said Jessi, finishing Mal's sentence. "In fact, that woman never even had a baby to begin with. What she told the dry cleaner was true — she doesn't have any children. The kid in her story was entirely made up."

We all laughed. "Wouldn't you know it?" asked Mary Anne. "Here was one time when the real story was even wilder than anyone could have imagined. And on top of it all, there was a happy ending."

I gazed across the room at Miriam, who was holding Daniel close as she stood in the middle of a half circle made up of my mom and my grandparents. How lucky it was that we had all come together again! Mary Anne was right. This story really did have a happy ending.

L. GODWIN

Ann M. Martin

About the Author

ANN MATTHEWS MARTIN was born on August 12, 1955. She grew up in Princeton, NJ, with her parents and her younger sister, Jane.

Although Ann used to be a teacher and then an editor of children's books, she's now a full-time writer. She gets the ideas for her books from many different places. Some are based on personal experiences. Others are based on childhood memories and feelings. Many are written about contemporary problems or events.

All of Ann's characters, even the members of the Baby-sitters Club, are made up. (So is Stoneybrook.) But many of her characters are based on real people. Sometimes Ann names her characters after people she knows, other times she chooses names she likes.

In addition to the Baby-sitters Club books, Ann Martin has written many other books for children. Her favorite is *Ten Kids, No Pets* because she loves big families and she loves animals. Her favorite Baby-sitters Club book is *Kristy's Big Day*. (By the way, Kristy is her favorite baby-sitter!)

Ann M. Martin now lives in New York with her cats, Gussie and Woody. Her hobbies are reading, sewing, and needlework — especially making clothes for children.

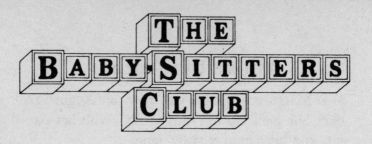

Look for Mystery #29

STACEY AND THE FASHION VICTIM

During Wednesday's fashion show, Harmony took a bad fall off the catwalk when a bright light flashed suddenly into her eyes. (She wasn't hurt, and she insisted she had fallen because she was wearing high heels — but I'd seen the lights.)

Another model broke out into a terrible, stinging rash after she'd applied some foundation from a jar she'd found on her dressing table.

And then there were the notes.

PRETTY IS AS PRETTY DOES UNTIL PRETTY DIES! said the one written in eyebrow pencil on the schedule posted on the dressing room door.

BEAUTY KILLS, said another, traced in some spilled face powder on one of the dressing tables.

And finally, in lip liner on one of the stalls in the girls' bathroom, MODEL BEHAVIOR CAN BE HAZARDOUS TO YOUR HEALTH.

Finally, Mrs. Maslin couldn't pretend it was all a joke anymore. She gathered all the models together after Wednesday's show (resort wear, as if it matters), and told us that she would do everything she could to make sure we were safe. She sounded very reassuring. But she also asked us to stay alert, and to be sure to report any suspicious behavior to her.

That night, I had a hard time hiding my fears from my mother. I couldn't believe she hadn't heard about what was going on; after all, she works at Bellair's. But this was her busiest season, and I knew she barely had a moment to herself.

For a second, over our dinner of takeout Chinese food, I had the impulse to tell her I wanted to quit. After all, modeling was fun, but it wasn't worth dying for.

Collect 'em all!

100 (and more) Reasons to Stay Friends Forever!

More titles... ➤

The Baby-sitters Club titles continued...

❑ MG48226-2	#82	Jessi and the Troublemaker	$3.99
❑ MG48235-1	#83	Stacey vs. the BSC	$3.50
❑ MG48228-9	#84	Dawn and the School Spirit War	$3.50
❑ MG48236-X	#85	Claudi Kishi, Live from WSTO	$3.50
❑ MG48227-0	#86	Mary Anne and Camp BSC	$3.50
❑ MG48237-8	#87	Stacey and the Bad Girls	$3.50
❑ MG22872-2	#88	Farewell, Dawn	$3.50
❑ MG22873-0	#89	Kristy and the Dirty Diapers	$3.50
❑ MG22874-9	#90	Welcome to the BSC, Abby	$3.99
❑ MG22875-1	#91	Claudia and the First Thanksgiving	$3.50
❑ MG22876-5	#92	Mallory's Christmas Wish	$3.50
❑ MG22877-3	#93	Mary Anne and the Memory Garden	$3.99
❑ MG22878-1	#94	Stacey McGill, Super Sitter	$3.99
❑ MG22879-X	#95	Kristy + Bart = ?	$3.99
❑ MG22880-3	#96	Abby's Lucky Thirteen	$3.99
❑ MG22881-1	#97	Claudia and the World's Cutest Baby	$3.99
❑ MG22882-X	#98	Dawn and Too Many Sitters	$3.99
❑ MG69205-4	#99	Stacey's Broken Heart	$3.99
❑ MG69206-2	#100	Kristy's Worst Idea	$3.99
❑ MG69207-0	#101	Claudia Kishi, Middle School Dropout	$3.99
❑ MG69208-9	#102	Mary Anne and the Little Princess	$3.99
❑ MG69209-7	#103	Happy Holidays, Jessi	$3.99
❑ MG45575-3		Logan's Story Special Edition Readers' Request	$3.25
❑ MG47118-X		Logan Bruno, Boy Baby-sitter	
		Special Edition Readers' Request	$3.50
❑ MG47756-0		Shannon's Story Special Edition	$3.50
❑ MG47686-6		The Baby-sitters Club Guide to Baby-sitting	$3.25
❑ MG47314-X		The Baby-sitters Club Trivia and Puzzle Fun Book	$2.50
❑ MG48400-1		BSC Portrait Collection: Claudia's Book	$3.50
❑ MG22864-1		BSC Portrait Collection: Dawn's Book	$3.50
❑ MG69181-3		BSC Portrait Collection: Kristy's Book	$3.99
❑ MG22865-X		BSC Portrait Collection: Mary Anne's Book	$3.99
❑ MG48399-4		BSC Portrait Collection: Stacey's Book	$3.50
❑ MG92713-2		The Complete Guide to The Baby-sitters Club	$4.95
❑ MG47151-1		The Baby-sitters Club Chain Letter	$14.95
❑ MG48295-5		The Baby-sitters Club Secret Santa	$14.95
❑ MG45074-3		The Baby-sitters Club Notebook	$2.50
❑ MG44783-1		The Baby-sitters Club Postcard Book	$4.95

Available wherever you buy books...or use this order form.
Scholastic Inc., P.O. Box 7502, 2931 E. McCarty Street, Jefferson City, MO 65102

Please send me the books I have checked above. I am enclosing $_____
(please add $2.00 to cover shipping and handling). Send check or money order–
no cash or C.O.D.s please.

Name_____ Birthdate_____

Address _____

City_____ State/Zip_____

BSC5962

THE BABY-SITTERS CLUB®

by Ann M. Martin

Collect and read these exciting BSC Super Specials, Mysteries, and Super Mysteries along with your favorite Baby-sitters Club books!

BSC Super Specials

❑ BBK44240-6	Baby-sitters on Board! Super Special #1	$3.95
❑ BBK44239-2	Baby-sitters' Summer Vacation Super Special #2	$3.95
❑ BBK43973-1	Baby-sitters' Winter Vacation Super Special #3	$3.95
❑ BBK42493-9	Baby-sitters' Island Adventure Super Special #4	$3.95
❑ BBK43575-2	California Girls! Super Special #5	$3.95
❑ BBK43576-0	New York, New York! Super Special #6	$4.50
❑ BBK44963-X	Snowbound! Super Special #7	$3.95
❑ BBK44962-X	Baby-sitters at Shadow Lake. Super Special #8	$3.95
❑ BBK45661-X	Starring The Baby-sitters Club! Super Special #9	$3.95
❑ BBK45674-1	Sea City, Here We Come! Super Special #10	$3.95
❑ BBK47015-9	The Baby-sitters Remember Super Special #11	$3.95
❑ BBK48308-0	Here Come the Bridesmaids! Super Special #12	$3.95
❑ BBK22883-8	Aloha, Baby-sitters! Super Special #13	$4.50

BSC Mysteries

❑ BAI44084-5	#1 Stacey and the Missing Ring	$3.50
❑ BAI44085-3	#2 Beware Dawn!	$3.50
❑ BAI44799-8	#3 Mallory and the Ghost Cat	$3.50
❑ BAI44800-5	#4 Kristy and the Missing Child	$3.50
❑ BAI44801-3	#5 Mary Anne and the Secret in the Attic	$3.50
❑ BAI44961-3	#6 The Mystery at Claudia's House	$3.50
❑ BAI44960-5	#7 Dawn and the Disappearing Dogs	$3.50
❑ BAI44959-1	#8 Jessi and the Jewel Thieves	$3.50
❑ BAI44958-3	#9 Kristy and the Haunted Mansion	$3.50
❑ BAI45696-2	#10 Stacey and the Mystery Money	$3.50

More titles ➡

The Baby-sitters Club books continued...

BSC Super Mysteries

Available wherever you buy books...or use this order form.

Scholastic Inc., P.O. Box 7502, 2931 East McCarty Street, Jefferson City, MO 65102-7502

Please send me the books I have checked above. I am enclosing $ _____
(please add $2.00 to cover shipping and handling). Send check or money order
— no cash or C.O.D.s please.

Name_____Birthdate_____

Address _____

City_____State/Zip_____

Please allow four to six weeks for delivery. Offer good in the U.S. only. Sorry, mail orders are not available to residents of Canada. Prices subject to change.

The New THE BABY-SITTERS CLUB® FAN CLUB

Only $8.95! Plus $2.00 Postage and Handling

Sign up now for a year of great friendships and terrific memories!

★ **110-mm camera!**
Take photos of your pals!

★ **Mini-photo album**
Fill it with your best pics!

★ **Diary (with lock!)**
For your favorite memories...and secret thoughts!

★ **Stationery note cards and stickers**
Send letters to your far-away friends!

★ **Eight cool pencils**
With the signatures of different baby-sitters!

★ **Full-color BSC poster**

★ **Subscription to the official BSC newsletter***

★ **Special keepsake shipper**

Amazing stuff!

To get your fan club pack (in the U.S. and Canada only), just fill out the coupon or write the information on a 3" x 5" card and send it to us with your check or money order. U.S. residents: $8.95 plus $2.00 postage and handling to The New BSC FAN CLUB, Scholastic Inc. P.O. Box 7500, 2931 East McCarty Street, Jefferson City, MO 65102. Canadian residents: $13.95 plus $2.00 postage and handling to The New BSC FAN CLUB, Scholastic Canada, 123 Newkirk Road, Richmond Hill, Ontario, L4C3G5. Offer expires 9/30/97. Offer good for one year from date of receipt. Please allow 4-6 weeks for your introductory pack to arrive.

*First newsletter is sent after introductory pack. You will receive at least 4 newsletters during your one-year membership.

- ✂ - -

Hurry! Send me my New Baby-sitters Club Fan Club Pack. I am enclosing my check or money order (no cash please) for U.S. residents: $10.95 ($8.95 plus $2.00) and for Canadian residents: $15.95 ($13.95 plus $2.00).

Name_____Birthdate_____
     First   Last   D/M/Y

Address_____

City_____State_____Zip_____

Telephone (   )_____Boy_____Girl_____

Where did you buy this book? ❑ Bookstore ❑ Book Fair ❑ Book Club ❑ Other_____

SCHOLASTIC

BM28297